CAT AND MOUSE

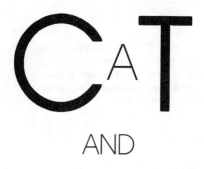

CAT

AND

MOUSE

A Brock Callahan Mystery

WILLIAM CAMPBELL GAULT

ST. MARTIN'S PRESS
New York

Design by Jaya Dayal

Library of Congress Cataloging-in-Publication Data

Gault, William Campbell.
    Cat and mouse/by William Campbell Gault.
       p. cm.
    ISBN 0-312-01398-1 : $12.95
    I. Title.
    PS3557.A948C3   1988
    813'.54—dc19   87-29936
                                                                      CIP

First Edition

10 9 8 7 6 5 4 3 2 1

FOR:

Ruth Cavin
Michael Congdon
Brian DeFiore
Marcia Muller
Bill Pronzini
All of the above helped to keep
this book from being stillborn.

CAT AND MOUSE

CHAPTER 1

THERE WAS AN ANCIENT BUT GLISTENING
bronze Camaro with mag wheels on our driveway when I
came home for lunch. I knew that car; it was Corey
Raleigh's, the town's youngest private investigator. He had
studied under me in a way; he had worked for me before
starting his own one-man agency in his parents' garage.

He was a lanky young man with a shrewd instinct for the
dollar and a fervent admiration for the fictional exploits of
Sam Spade, Philip Marlowe, and Lew Archer.

He was in the kitchen, talking with our housekeeper, Mrs.
Casey, his surrogate mother.

"Long time no see," I said.

"I've been in Los Angeles," he explained, "on a case.
Man, that's where the action is, right?"

"Right. That's why I moved up here."

Mrs. Casey said, "If you two are going to talk shop, why
don't you talk it out on the deck? I'll bring our lunch out
there."

Mrs. Casey does not approve of the trade I had practiced
in Los Angeles. Nor is she happy about the fact that Corey
now practiced it here in San Valdesto.

We sat in back under the shade of the overhang next to
the pool. I said, "Your fame must have spread if they called
you from L.A."

He shook his head. "My aunt has a cassette and record store in North Hollywood that's been robbed a lot. All I did down there was play night-watchman."

"And that's what you call action?"

"Of course not! But I had my days free and I made the rounds of some of the agencies down there. Boy, the stories those guys told me!"

"I'm sure at least three percent of them were true. Did you apprehend any burglars?"

He nodded. "Kids, punks. I hated to turn 'em in." He paused. "I wondered if you had anything going that you needed help on. Things have been kind of slow at the office."

I shook my head. "Remember, I'm retired, Corey."

His smile was cynical. "Sure you are. That's why you renewed your license this spring."

Then Mrs. Casey came with our lunch, beef stroganoff. For Corey she serves beef stroganoff; for the master of the house it is usually a ham-and-cheese sandwich.

We sat and ate and talked of other things, in deference to Mrs. Casey. Then she went to her room for the first of her daytime dramas on the boob tube and I walked with Corey to the front door.

I closed the door and was two steps away from it when it opened again. Corey stepped back in and said, "There's a cat on your front lawn and I think it's dead." He pointed at a spot at the far end of the driveway.

We walked there together. It was a sleek and slender cat of pale fawn, blue-eyed and short-haired, with darker ears, paws, tail, and face. It was dead; its throat had been cut.

"Jesus!" Corey said. "Some son-of-a-bitch–– It's a Siamese, isn't it?"

I nodded. "Some kinky kid, probably. Look, don't tell Jan about this, or Mrs. Casey. I'll dump it in the trash can. It's collection day."

"What kind of kid would do this?"

I shrugged. I could see the collection truck at the far

2

end of the road. I picked up the cat by its tail and put it in the half-filled trash can and buried it with clippings from the full one.

Corey suggested, "Maybe one of the neighbors saw who put it there. Maybe you ought to ask them."

I shook my head. "It would get back to Jan. Forget it."

"Never!" he said.

I didn't have to ask the neighbors. One of them, Bill Crider, was coming across the street toward me as Corey's car pulled away.

He told me, "I saw you put that cat in the can just now. I thought, when I saw the car go by, it was one of those throwaway newspaper peddlers. If I'd known what it was I would have got his license number."

"What kind of car was it?"

"An old Plymouth two-door sedan, gray. It had a rumpled left rear fender. Thank God, Sally isn't home. She's a cat lover."

Sally is his wife. I said, "You'd better not mention it to her. The cat's throat was cut."

He stared at me. "What kind of creep would— Should we go looking for him? He could still be in the neighborhood. It only happened about ten minutes ago."

"He must be long gone by now," I said. "He sure as hell wouldn't dump it in his own neighborhood. And there aren't many people driving old Plymouths in this neighborhood, Bill."

He nodded. "That's for sure. But there have been two houses burglarized up here in the last week. Maybe we ought to start a neighborhood watch."

"Maybe. I'll phone Sheriff McClune. He's a friend of mine. Did you get a good look at the driver?"

He shook his head. "Damn it, no." He sighed. "We moved up here from L.A. just to get away from this kind of thing. This was going to be our sanctuary for our senior years."

3

"I'll phone the sheriff," I repeated.

"Okay," he said dully. "But I still think we should start a neighborhood watch."

A sanctuary for seniors. I hadn't reached that plateau yet; I would have to wait for my sanctuary. Since Hiroshima the only guaranteed sanctuary was the grave.

I phoned the sheriff's station and McClune was in. I told him what had happened.

"Brock," he said in an even voice, "we are currently investigating two burglaries in your neck of the woods and you phone me about a dead cat."

"The cat's throat was cut," I explained. "Don't you think that might indicate the guy is a weirdo?"

"Yes," he said wearily. "An old gray Plymouth two-door sedan with a rumpled left rear fender? I'll put out the word. When are we going to play poker again?"

"As soon as Bernie arranges another game."

"Maybe we ought to have one without Bernie. He *always* wins!"

"Not always. I nailed him for three hundred one night."

"I remember," he said. "That was eighteen months ago. But hell, we need him, don't we? We need the challenge."

"We do. He teaches us humility."

Lieutenant Bernard Vogel of the San Valdesto Police Department was another of my cop friends. Unfortunately, he is more cop than friend, which is endemic among the boys in blue when they deal with private eyes—or former private eyes. I had learned that in my maiden years in Los Angeles.

The mist began to drift in at about three o'clock. It was a dense fog when Jan got home. It had been a slow and dangerous trip for her down the curving pass from Solvang, she told me, where she had gone to see a client. Jan is an interior decorator working for Kay Décor.

"And what's new on the home front?" she asked when I brought her her drink.

"Nothing exciting. I was talking with Bill Crider this afternoon. He thinks we ought to have a neighborhood watch."

4

"Because of those two homes that were burglarized?"

"Yup."

"They were daylight burglaries," she informed me. "The prevailing opinion is that they were high school kids."

I hadn't known that. I don't read the local paper.

"At the noon hour, the lunch hour," she explained. "And what did they steal? No jewelry, no bonds, no paintings, no antiques. Only the cash they found."

"They must have been kids," I agreed.

She sipped her martini. I took a swallow of my beer. I asked, "Do you remember that cat you had when we were courting?"

She nodded.

"Was it a Siamese?"

She shook her head. "A Burmese. They look a lot alike. What brought this on?"

"Nostalgia, I guess. I was thinking . . . we don't have a cat or a dog, not even a canary."

"All we have is us," she said, "us and Mrs. Casey. Isn't that enough?"

"I guess. But the way things are going these days I've been thinking maybe a mean Doberman wouldn't be a bad investment."

She smiled. "You and your nyctophobia! Turn on the tube and let's see what's going on in Tinsel Town."

We caught the opening news story on Channel 2 in Los Angeles. The creature known as the Valley Intruder had entered another home in that area, raping and strangling a seventy-nine-year-old widow. That ran his police estimate to fourteen rapes or murders or both.

"Turn it off," Jan said, "and make me another martini."

"Coming up," I said. "Do you notice that the creep invades only those homes that leave a door or a window unlocked?"

"Yes, macho man. But we have you for that, don't we?"

I gave her my injured husband look and went to get her another martini. I have this chauvinistic feeling that if we

5

ever get the women's-rights movement rightfully established in this free country we maligned males might finally achieve equality.

We watched "Masterpiece Theatre" on the PBS channel after dinner in the den. Mrs. Casey watched a rerun of *High Noon* on the tube in her room. Mrs. Casey has cinematic taste; she stays with the golden oldies.

The day's restlessness didn't invade the night. I slept soundly, all the doors and windows locked.

Larry Rubin, my bookie, phoned me when we were eating breakfast. He had a hot one, a cinch, running in the sixth at Santa Anita, he informed me. Did I want a piece of the action?

I told him to put me down for a double sawbuck, and asked, "How's it going with you these days?"

"Great! I'll be back to my Cadillac days in another month."

"Maybe even a Mercedes?"

"Jews who buy German cars," he informed me cooly, "have no memories."

"Sorry, Larry. No offense meant."

"And none taken. Any goy who lends me five grand and doesn't even charge interest has to be a brother. By the way, I was down in L.A. over the weekend and stopped in at Heinie's. He told me there was some guy down there asking about you. He wanted to know where you had moved to. Heinie told him he didn't know. I guess he didn't like the looks of the guy."

"I'm glad. Heinie is a great judge of character. Let me know if I win, *brother.*"

"Natch!"

When I came back to the kitchen Jan asked, "Who was that?"

"Larry Rubin. He has a hot one running at Santa Anita. I told him I'd go for twenty on the nag."

"I'll take ten of it. Okay?"

"Yes. Cash, please?" Jan likes to win but resents paying. She sighed. She got up and went into the living room to get her purse. She came back and handed me a ten-dollar bill. I decided not to tell her what Larry had said about German cars. Jan runs a Mercedes.

It was at Heinie's, my favorite bar and grille, that I had met Larry Rubin. He was a horse player then, not a bookie. The boys and girls at Heinie's called him The Wizard Of Odds.

Nobody, they claimed, could rate a horse or a jock or a track or any significant combination of the three as accurately as Larry. I agreed with that. Larry was the only horse player I'd ever known that bookies tried to avoid.

Unfortunately, like all mortals, Larry had a grandiose view of his skills in other fields of wagering. So he would go to Vegas when he was overly flush and try his skill at blackjack, poker, and roulette.

As any sane gambler knows, Las Vegas is the last place to go if you want to beat the odds. The houses in Vegas arrange their own bizarre odds and they are not designed to give the sucker a break. Suckers are what keep them in business. That is why they court the convention trade. Winners are not welcome in Nevada.

It was when his great gift at picking winners began to fade that Larry decided to move over to the other side of his profession. But Los Angeles is a highly competitive bookie area. He came up here after his last trip to Vegas, along with his bride of two weeks, a Vegas chorus girl. He came up broke. I lent him five thousand dollars for seed money; he paid me back in four months.

I had insisted on the no-interest bit; Larry's tips had kept me eating in the early days of my chosen trade after leaving the Rams. Owing and being owed; I believe in that.

I waited until Jan went to work before phoning Heinie at his home number. His bar didn't open until eleven.

7

"Well, stranger!" he said. "It's about time! I thought you'd died."

"Not yet. Larry Rubin told me this morning that some man was asking about me down there."

"Yeh. Probably a bill collector. I told him I wasn't sure where you were now, the last I'd heard it was Patagonia. He was a mean-looking bastard, a big guy."

"No further description?"

"About two hundred and forty pounds, bald. He had a scar running down his right cheek from just below the eye almost to his chin."

"It doesn't ring a bell with me. I put away some mean hoodlums but never one with a scar like that."

"So, maybe it was a fan. You still married to Jan?"

"Of course!"

"Treat her right. You are one lucky man."

"I know. Keep the faith, Heinie."

"Faith in what? Today? Shit!"

My sentiments exactly (almost). I took a cup of coffee out to the deck along with the sports pages from the morning paper. I left the rest of the paper on the breakfast-nook table for Mrs. Casey. She does windows but not breakfasts and has made it clear that she desires privacy when she eats hers.

As I had told Heinie, I had been instrumental in putting some rough characters behind bars when I was working the mean streets of Los Angeles. I'd had several threatening letters from a couple of them when they left prison.

But I would have remembered a man who fit the description Heinie had given me. It couldn't have been a bill collector. I'd paid off every debt I had in town when my Uncle Homer died and made me solvent enough to retire and move up here.

It had probably been a fan. I still had a couple of those left.

CHAPTER 2

IN THE FORMER CHAUFFEUR'S QUARTERS above the garage, the file cabinet I had brought up from Los Angeles was still intact. The history of my adventures in Tinsel Town were all recorded there. The cabinet was covered with dust; the files were dustless enough to bring into Mrs. Casey's house.

I took them down to the den in two trips. I had not become rich in Los Angeles but I certainly had been busy.

Some current sage was recently quoted as saying, "Nostalgia ain't what it used to be." These files were.

My modest second-floor office had been in Beverly Hills. There were some memorable names in the files: directors and actors and producers, boxers and football players, two heiresses and one starlet who only last week imprinted her hands in the cement walk of Hollywood Boulevard.

On the seamier side of the law, the files were fewer and older. These were the rough guys, the victims of my code of vindictive retribution. Many of their names brought back memories but not one resembled the man Heinie had described.

I was putting the files away in a cabinet for further consideration when the phone rang. It was Bernie. He said, "McClune tells me you're aching to play poker again."

"He lied. It was his idea."

"So, why don't you take me to some expensive place for lunch and we can discuss it?"

"What a vulgar, mercenary suggestion!"

"Okay. I just thought you might still believe in your own code."

"Which is?"

"Owing and being owed."

"You're right, I owe you. Pierre's?"

"Why not? He has your kind of food, too. Hamburger."

"He calls it Salisbury steak."

"I know. All you have to do is to tell him you want the Salisbury steak without the egg, bread crumbs, and seasoning."

"I'll do that. Twelve-thirty?"

"I'll be there. And don't forget to wear a tie."

"Twelve-thirty," I repeated.

I did owe Bernie. He had covered for me in all my local escapades and backed me against Chief Chandler Harris. And he had alerted some of his gambling peers to the only bookie in town who paid track odds on long shots, Larry Rubin. Like Larry, Bernie wouldn't drive a German car if they were five cents a copy, tax included.

I figured I owed it to Pierre to dress with some decorum. I wore my gray flannel slacks with a charcoal jacket and a white oxford shirt. As a minor protest against the absurdity of his demanding a tie even for *lunch* (in California?) I put on a Mickey Mouse tie that one of my Little Leaguers had brought back for me after his visit to Disneyland.

Pierre's is in Montevista, a suburb of San Valdesto. I was about to pull into a parking space near the entrance when I saw an old gray two-door Plymouth sedan at the far end of the lot. I drove down and parked in the vacant space next to it.

Neither rear fender was crumpled, but the left one could have been hammered out and repainted. The paint in one spot on it seemed to be newer. It was obviously smoother.

10

The right side door was not locked. I opened it and reached into the car, opened the glove compartment, and took out the registration slip. I was reading it when a shrill voice from the other end of the lot called, "Get away from that car, you damned thief!"

A pair of stout and middle-aged women were bearing down on me from the restaurant entrance. I replaced the slip, closed the car door, and put on my winningest smile.

When they came within range, I said, "I apologize, ma'am. I thought it was my wife's car. We've been . . . well, I don't want to go into that. I assure you I am not a thief. I am meeting a police officer here for lunch. He will be glad to confirm what I told you."

She glared at me. "A likely story! We're not waiting for *anybody*. Get out of here! Go back where you came from."

"Sorry," I said with hauteur, "but I have a reservation for lunch, and my officer friend will soon be here to meet me." I nodded a curt good-bye and walked away.

Bernie was waiting for me under the canvas canopy in front of the restaurant door when I got there. He apparently had not witnessed the squalid scene and I didn't see any reason to mention it. He looked at my tie, sadly shook his head, and said nothing.

Pierre met us at the door, sadly shook his head and looked at Bernie. "Maybe a corner table where nobody will notice him?" Bernie suggested.

"In which case," I said, "Lieutenant Vogel will pick up the tab."

"This way, gentlemen," Pierre said. He led us to a table where we had a view of the town below and the sea beyond it.

Bernie ordered a dry martini, I a beaker of draft Einlicher.

Pierre said, "I owe you a lot, Mr. Callahan, for introducing me to that beer. Today, I will instruct my chef to broil you the finest hamburger you have ever tasted."

"Thank you," I said.

"And don't forget his ketchup," Bernie said. "I'll order later."

Pierre smiled and left. Bernie said, "What's this about the cat on your lawn? McClune mentioned it."

I gave him the sordid story.

"A kid, maybe?" he asked. "They've had a lot of juvenile burglaries in Montevista. And the ones they caught weren't poor kids. But papa doesn't give them a big enough allowance to pay for their dope."

"I doubt if this was a kid." I told him about the man who had asked about me at Heinie's.

He frowned. "I don't see the connection."

"Neither do I, yet." I shrugged. "You know me. I work on instinct."

"Don't downgrade it," he told me. "I've seen it at work. Have you been threatened before by people you put away?"

"A couple of times. Have you?"

He nodded. "Oh, yes! And they included some vicious remarks about my heritage."

When we had finished our drinks, Bernie ordered something in French I can't spell and the waiter assured me I was in for a delicious surprise, compliments of Pierre. Way down deep in his devious soul I have the feeling that Pierre likes me and forgives all big tippers.

The hamburger the waiter brought me was large and pristine. He brought the ketchup along to make it less pristine. Bernie's plate made me wonder if it was possible Pierre's septic tank had overflown again. All sauce, no chow, French cuisine.

I am not a complete lout. I tried the hamburger without the ketchup. Delicious! I made the thought vocal.

"It's probably gourmet-grade chopped filet," Bernie informed me. "You're lucky it's on the house." He took a sip of his wine; I took a sip of my second Einlicher. He said, "I told McClune I would alert the patrol boys in town about that gray Plymouth. I'm sure no kid in your area is driving one of those unless it's a classic."

"It isn't."

"Now, about the poker. Is Saturday night at my house okay with you?"

"I guess. Unless Jan has other plans. How much money should I bring?"

"Whatever you can afford. I can arrange transportation for you if you need it."

"No, thanks. It will be worth the trip just to see Ellie again. What is she doing these days?"

Ellie is his wife. He shrugged. "I'm not sure if it's saving the whales or fighting that oil company that wants to drill off Omega Beach or writing nasty letters to our governor. That woman—"

"Is a citizen," I finished for him. "That's getting to be an archaic word, isn't it?"

"Could you define it for me?"

"Yes. It is a voter who quite often votes against his or her own self-interest."

He smiled. "Could you name one?"

"It would be immodest of me. What do you want for dessert?"

"I've cost you enough already," he said. "Only coffee for me."

"You have just become a citizen," I told him.

My good friend and occasional adversary, Bernie Vogel. We are different breeds of cat but I admire him. He could have retired five years ago on the property in town his father had left him. But I am sure he felt it was his citizen's duty to put the bad guys where they belong (in the can or under the sod) and to maintain an orderly world. As a student of history he should have realized that there hadn't been an orderly world since the dawn of civilization.

There was still a lot of afternoon left. I drove back and forth in the lower Main Street district on the off chance I might spot an old gray Plymouth two-door sedan with a crumpled left rear fender. The area was loaded with old cars and crumpled fenders but not one of them was a gray Plymouth two-door sedan. I went home.

Mrs. Casey had brought in the mail. It was on the table in the front hall: one letter, two bills, and nine pieces of junk mail. I opened the letter and read it.

Then I phoned Bernie. "You can forget Saturday night," I told him. "I'll be staying at home for a while. I just got a letter."

"What kind of letter?"

"Seven words—'The cat was first. Who is second?'"

"Take it to McClune," he said. "They've got a better lab up there and a much faster computerized fingerprint file."

"I'm not leaving the house."

"Okay. I'll phone him and have him send a deputy to pick it up. Sit tight, buddy."

I phoned Corey's office and he was there. "Are you still available for night work?" I asked him.

"Hell, yes. A store?"

"No. Our house. Did you get your gun permit?"

"Six months ago. What in hell is going on, Brock?"

"I'll tell you when you get here. Take a nap now and come around ten o'clock. Bring the gun."

"Right!"

I still had the second-hand gun I bought in Los Angeles when I opened the office. I had carried it on only two cases there. It was an ancient .38-caliber Colt Police Special. The gun was still in working order but the ammunition for it had been discarded years ago. I could get more; guns and ammunition are easy to buy in this country, too easy.

I was going over my files again when the doorbell rang. Mrs. Casey got there the same time I did.

The deputy said, "I came for the letter."

I handed it to him and he left. Mrs. Casey asked, "What's happening, Mr. Callahan? The Criders' maid told me this afternoon that somebody threw a dead cat on our lawn. And now this!"

14

"Patience," I said. "I'll explain it all when Jan comes home."

"I don't like it," she said.

"I don't either, Mrs. Casey. Let's wait for Jan."

She went back to the kitchen muttering to herself. I went back to my files. Nothing, nothing, nothing . . .

The phone rang. It was Larry. He said, "I've got a hundred and forty dollars here for you. Do you want to pick it up or should I bring it over?"

"Not today. Mail me a check. Mail two checks, seventy of it to Jan the other seventy to me."

"Mail? What's with you? Trouble, Brock?"

"Yes."

"Is it connected with that guy asking about you at Heinie's?"

"I don't know. It's possible."

"I've still got some friends down there, chum, who are on the shady side. You call me if you think they could be useful."

"Thanks. I'll do that."

Occasionally giving me an inside tip on a hot one and booking my bet was Larry's way of paying the interest I had refused. It was possible, of course, that Larry laid off my bet as he did with his own money down in Los Angeles. Today's sixth could have been a boat race, but that seemed highly unlikely at Santa Anita.

Jan came home a little after five o'clock and we gathered in the living room. I related all that had happened, starting with the dead cat and finishing with today's letter.

When I had finished, Jan said, "So that's why you were asking about my cat." She looked at Mrs. Casey. "Did you know about it?"

"Not until this afternoon when the Criders' maid told me."

Jan looked at me. "And that's why Bill Crider wants a neighborhood watch?"

15

"No. It's the burglaries he's concerned about. What I would like to suggest is that you girls take a suite at the Biltmore and live it up while I watch the house."

"No way!" Jan said.

"I second the motion," Mrs. Casey said.

"I was afraid of that," I said, "so I phoned Corey. He'll guard us nights, I'll be home during the day. Could we take a vote on that?"

Jan looked at Mrs. Casey and she nodded.

Jan said, "And now I think we should have a quiet drink."

"I'll get my Irish whiskey," Mrs. Casey said. "It will be nice to have Corey in the house."

. . .*where she can finally convert him to the true faith*, I thought, *and he can learn to play bingo.* I didn't voice the thought.

The man asking about me at Heinie's and the dead cat on the lawn might have been only a coincidence. But the dead cat on the lawn and the seven-word letter certainly was not.

And why had the writer added, "Who is second?" Someone other than Callahan? My Jan? Why hadn't he written "next"? Had he planned more than two? Trying to analyze the mind of a kook was traveling down a trail too murky for me.

We played gin rummy after dinner, loser sits out, and Mrs. Casey won, as usual. Jan said she didn't have any small bills in her purse. Mrs. Casey said she could make change for a large one. Jan said I wouldn't mind paying for her. I was not consulted on that decision.

Then Mrs. Casey went up to her room to watch a Bogart rerun and Jan went in the den to watch a PBS program on the Aztec civilization. I went out into the gloom and sat in a deck chair on the front lawn, waiting for Corey to show.

I could hear the twin tail pipes of his Camaro rumbling long before the car came into sight around the bend of the hill.

He had brought his lunch box with him, complete with a

16

vacuum bottle in the lid. Night watches were what paid most of the rent in his new one-room office downtown.

In the living room, the area of my previous seminar, I told him what I had told Jan and Mrs. Casey.

"A live one for a change," he said. "I hope the bastard shows up on my watch."

"Corey," I admonished him, "you must remember that we are not the law."

"We're a damned sight closer to it than he is. Stop fretting, Brock. I'm a big boy now."

He showed me his revolver, what the local police were carrying since they had switched from Colt, a .38-caliber Smith & Wesson.

He had brought a box of ammo along and they would fit my ancient Colt. He gave me a dozen from the box. I took them to the bedroom and stored them on the highest shelf in the closet, deep in the corner, next to my gun. Guns make me almost as nervous as gun owners do. My policeman father had been killed by a hoodlum's gun when I was twelve years old.

Our living room is in the front of the house. That is where Corey would sit and watch through the huge picture window. I turned the lawn lights on.

Mrs. Casey came down during a commercial to ask him if he would like a snack. He told her he had brought it. She went back to Bogart.

The mist drifted in before Jan and I went to bed, shrouding the lawn lights, obscuring the view of the road.

We didn't stay up for the eleven-o'clock news; we had our own troubles now.

CHAPTER 3

IT WAS A RESTLESS NIGHT. I DREAMED OF MY father again. Jan slept on; my mate has a less violent history. In the morning, at breakfast, she said she had decided not to go to work today.

"I can drive you down," Corey offered. "You're safe with me."

She shook her head. "It's not that. Fiesta starts tomorrow and all the tourists are already in town."

"There might be some customers among them," I pointed out.

"For Kay Décor?" She made a face. "Hardly! Practically all of the better shops are closing for the weekend."

Better is Jan's euphemism for *expensive.*

Corey left, after his second helping of pancakes, and Jan went out to the pool. I sat in the living room, reading a Muller-Pronzini mystery, but facing the window so I could keep an eye on the road.

The cars went by. The only old ones were classics, a 1930 Duesenberg, a 1965 Mustang, an ancient Stutz Bearcat. The new ones were mostly Porsches and Cads and Continentals—and a county patrol car. The patrol car cruised slowly past twice.

McClune phoned around ten-thirty to tell me they had

18

come up with zilch; no definable fingerprints and the stationery was available at any cheap chain store.

"Probably some smogtown weirdo," he said. "Do you have a record of your cases down there?"

"Yes. And I've gone over them three times."

"Well," McClune said, "we're patrolling that area more than usual. There was another burglary yesterday. Maybe we scared him away."

"I hope not. I want that bastard!"

"Easy, Brock!"

"Sorry. I criticized Corey for saying almost the same thing last night. We are not the law."

"Exactly. Though I must admit you've helped the law here since you moved up."

"Thank you."

"You're welcome. I'll keep in touch."

The law in San Vadesto, both county and city, had been more tolerant of me than it had been in Los Angeles. The cynical thought came to me that I was now richer than I had been in Los Angeles. The sensible thought came to me that I should not look a gift horse in the mouth.

"You're mumbling again," a voice said.

It was Jan, wearing a terry-cloth robe over her bikini.

"Again?"

She nodded. "You woke me up twice last night. Why don't you go out to the pool and get some exercise? I'll sit here."

I put on my trunks and went out to swim a leisurely ten laps. Though now solvent and snug in suburbia, I was still the punk who had been on probation for one full year in his Long Beach youth, a hot-rodder, son of a cop father and an angelic mother, Stanford graduate, my jersey in the Hall of Fame at Canton. And now I was being held house-bound by a creepy cat killer. . . . Who wouldn't mumble?

I worked on the weights for half an hour, took a shower, and it was time for lunch.

19

Mrs. Casey ate with us. "How long is this going to last?" she asked.

"I don't know."

Jan said, "If it keeps up too long I'll go stir crazy."

I nodded. "That's why I suggested the Biltmore."

I finished the Muller-Pronzini book after lunch and went out to turn on the lawn sprinklers. Across the street, Bill and Sally Crider were talking to a man I recognized as a local realtor.

The Criders went into the house; the realtor came over to ask, "How's it going, Brock?"

"Fair enough. Are the Criders putting their house up for sale?"

He nodded. "This area's turning into a battle zone. How about you?"

"It might be hard to sell," I explained, "if I told the buyers my reason for moving. And that would be the only decent thing to do, wouldn't it?"

He smiled. "Same old acid tongue! A man has to eat, Brock."

"Even cannibals," I admitted.

"Even cannibals," he agreed. "Have a nice day, Brock."

He smiled again, nodded a good-bye, walked to his BMW parked across the street, and went away.

Constant smilers give me the chills. Those millionaire television preachers who appeal to the right-wing red-necks infesting our country quote their personal interpretations of the Bible, rationalize their bigotries—and never stop smiling. The bland face of evil . . .

One thing you can say about big bald mean guys who kill cats, they don't try to look holy.

The patrol car cruised by again before I went into the house. Jan was talking on the phone to Audrey Kay, her boss. Mrs. Casey had come to the kitchen to stack the lunch dishes in the washer. Her next daytime drama was not due for half an hour.

I took a bottle of Einlicher out of the fridge and settled down in the living room to read the latest Travis McGee. I was halfway through it when Corey arrived.

"My folks aren't home," he explained, "and I thought you wouldn't mind a fourth at dinner."

"I'm sure Mrs. Casey won't. Which reminds me, we never discussed your current rates."

He looked embarrassed, the first time I had ever seen that look on his face. "Gee, Brock, I don't know—"

"You can't afford any freebies," I told him sternly. "You're a professional now."

He shrugged. "My aunt gave me six and a half dollars an hour in L.A."

"That's for family. I'll make it seven."

He shook his head. "You're family, too. I'll settle for six."

Corey is not one of those modern restless young men who leave home for their own bachelor apartment as soon as they start to shave. He has economic sense; he knows that he can get better cooking, free laundry, and more comfortable quarters at a much more reasonable price with his doting parents.

He had gone to school at the local UCSV and lived at home even then. As a matter of fact, he had shared his room (but not his meals) with a classmate and generously split with his parents the rent his friend paid him.

After dinner, Corey went up to watch another Bogart picture with Mrs. Casey. Jan and I sat in the living room, the lawn lights on, me with McGee, she with the current *New York Review of Books*.

Around nine-thirty, a car stopped in front. I turned off the lights in the living room; the headlights on the car went out.

The front door light at the Criders' went on, the door opened, and Bill was outlined in the glow from behind him. Both the Crider cars were on the driveway; it was probably the reason the stranger's car had parked in front of our house.

"Who is it?" Jan asked.

A man and a woman came into view on the Criders' walkway. "It could be a real estate salesman and his customer. The Criders have their house up for sale."

"At this time of night?"

"I guess they're in a hurry to move."

I turned on the lights again and went back to McGee. Jan went into the den and turned on the tube, an opiate for the masses that had not been foreseen by kooky Karl.

I joined her in there when Corey came down to take up his watch.

She sighed. "I never felt this nervous in Los Angeles."

"That was a different time and place then and we were younger. This won't last forever."

I drank a glass of warm milk before going to bed; my ulcer was acting up again. Patience has never been one of my virtues. Like the renowned Arnold Palmer, I hate to *wait!*

My night was less troubled than the previous night's and dreamless. Jan slept soundly, thanks to the sedative she had taken.

At breakfast, Corey said, "That guy might be out of town by now. It could have been his dumb idea of a joke."

"I doubt it. Let's give it a couple more days."

"And then move to Paris," Jan said.

Mrs. Casey had joined us for breakfast this morning. She shook her head. "I'm not running from something the likes of *him!* I still have my late husband's hunting knife. I keep it on the table right next to the bed."

My kind of woman, Mrs. Casey. She asks for no quarter and grants none.

The wind had shifted; the day was sunny. My friends at the golf course would be looking for me, the pigeon who kept them solvent. I phoned one of the pirates and told him I would not be able to join them today.

He expressed deep regret, though I am sure it was more monetary than sentimental. Gambling golfers can afford camaraderie but not compassion.

No golf, no poker, no freedom, held in house bondage by a

22

puke who could be in Cucamonga by now, a man in the shadows who didn't have enough guts to come out into the open, a man playing cat-and-mouse—and I was the 228-pound mouse. Though I had apologized to McClune and admonished Corey, *I wanted that bastard!*

I went back to my files. A man could have turned bald since last we met, a man could get his face scarred. I went through the hoodlum files, sorting out the heavyweights, the ones I could remember. Bush leaguers, most of them, burglary, assault, theft. This was before I had started to get the carriage trade. The ones I remembered didn't shape up as likely suspects for the game the shadow man was playing.

I went to the kitchen for another glass of milk before lunch. Mrs. Casey had brought in the mail. There were only four pieces of junk mail today. There was one piece of first-class mail; two checks, each for seventy dollars, one made out to Jan, one to me, compliments of Larry Rubin.

Jan's smile was rueful. "Maybe it's a lucky omen."

"Maybe. I'll eat in the living room. Nothing heavy, though. My stomach is acting up."

"So is mine. Patience, Brock." She kissed me. "We mustn't panic. That only makes us more vulnerable."

Chicken soup, cheese and crackers, that was my lunch. Then Jan came in to tell me she would keep watch in the living room. "You need the exercise more than I do," she explained. "And maybe it will help to calm you."

I shook my head. "I'll go out and nap in the shade. I'm really bushed. I suppose it's frustration."

"And rage," she added. "How about a sedative?"

"No. Not yet."

"My macho man," she said. "I almost hope, for his sake, the police find that cat killer before you do."

I dozed on a chaise longue in the shade but sleep wouldn't come. I sat in the shallow end of the sun warmed pool, the water up to my chin. This was better. Some of the tension

23

eased in my shoulder muscles, my stomach returned to near normal.

Both the county and the city police had been alerted; something had to break in a town this size. But then I remembered it was Fiesta week. The town would be jammed with tourists. The city police would have more problems than usual with traffic control, invading sharpies, and drunks. They would need all the help they could get from the sheriff's department. The restaurants, the motels and hotels, the liquor stores would be coining it; the police would be overworked.

This was a vacation town for the tourists, a supposed sanctuary for the retired citizens who lived here. The Criders hadn't found it to be enough of a sanctuary to make them comfortable. Even high-school burglars had panicked them.

Day after day in this fair country the underprivileged in our big cities face violence and hunger, insult and injury, ghetto fires and racial wars. While the suburbanites fret about taxes, our vicious crabgrass invasion, and a declining water supply for our swimming pools. Maybe it was our turn to suffer.

Over our drinks before dinner Jan said, "You feel better now, don't you?"

"Saner, maybe. More angry than scared."

"You were scared for Mrs. Casey and me, weren't you? I've never seen you scared before."

"I have been."

"But this time it was for us, wasn't it?"

"I guess. Should we have another drink?"

"I'll make them."

I went out after dinner and circled the house, checking the shrubs that fronted the windows, looking for footprints in the loose soil in which they were planted. There were four sides to the house; an intruder could approach from any of the neighboring yards.

Then Jan and I sat in the living room, she with the local

evening paper, I trying to balance my checkbook. Arithmetic had never been my strong suit and my present state of mind was not rational enough to make it any easier. It had become more complicated to figure since my Uncle Homer died. Before my inheritance the bank had been kind enough to keep me informed about my daily balance every time I was overdrawn.

I had it balanced within a few dollars by nine o'clock. That was close enough for me. I put some golden oldies on the record player, Dixieland jazz, turned the volume low so as not to bother Jan, and stared out at the full moon.

Ten o'clock came and Corey had not arrived. Corey and I share this old-fashioned belief that a ten- or five- or two-o'clock promise means *exactly* that. One minute after any promised time is a broken promise.

It was possible that his ancient Camaro had failed him. But that was hard to believe; he kept it in top mechanical shape. At a quarter after ten I phoned his house.

His father told me he had left early, over an hour ago. "Call me when he gets there, won't you, Mr. Callahan?"

"I will. Maybe he ran out of gas or had a flat tire."

"Maybe. Call me."

The phone rang two minutes later. It was Corey. He said, "I'm being held at the sheriff's station. I know you can't leave the house, but could you send somebody?"

"Yes. What are you being held for?"

"Murder," he said.

CHAPTER 4

"**W**HAT HAPPENED?"

"Brock," he said wearily. "I'm too groggy to talk. I was knocked out. Just send somebody!"

I knew a lot of high-priced lawyers in town, most of whom played golf. But murder was no case for golfing lawyers. I phoned Stan Nowicki.

"I know it's late," I apologized. "But Corey Raleigh is being held at the sheriff's station and, for reasons I'll explain later, I can't go up there now. Would you?"

"Of course. What's the charge?"

"Murder."

"Corey Raleigh—?"

"That's what he told me."

"Are you going to stay up? The station isn't far from your house and I could drop in on my way home."

"I'll be up."

I phoned Mr. Raleigh and told him what I had told Stan. I added, "I've sent my attorney up there. It has to be some kind of mistake. I'll keep you informed."

"Don't bother," he said. "I'll go up there and find out for myself."

Jan had overheard both conversations. She said, "I think you should go there, Brock."

26

I shook my head. "It could be a ploy to get me out of the house. Stan Nowicki is going to stop here on his way home. He'll have the story. Let's not tell Mrs. Casey about it, not yet."

She nodded in agreement. "Corey—? Murder? That's crazy!"

"It could be a frame," I said. "He told me he'd been knocked out."

"Do you think it was that man who—who—"

"Threw the cat on our lawn?" I finished for her. "It could be. Let's wait for Stan."

We were sitting in the living room, staring out the front window, when Mrs. Casey came in to ask, "Where's Corey?"

Jan looked at me. I said, "He's in some trouble at the sheriff's station. We're not sure what it is. I sent Nowicki up there to find out."

Mrs. Casey sighed. "I'll make some coffee."

We sat and sipped and stared. At eleven-thirty, Jan said, "Maybe you'd better call the station."

I shook my head. "Stan will be here."

He was with us fifteen minutes later. He sat on the couch next to Jan and said, "I'll give you the department's version first."

A sheriff's patrol car had been cruising the road we live on. About a mile and a half up the slope from our house the deputy saw an old gray Plymouth parked below a deserted cabin some distance from the road. He had called for backup. When it arrived they used the bullhorn for warning, got no response, and charged the house. Inside, they found Corey just gaining consciousness, his gun still in his hand. And they found the dead man, a large rock in his hand stained with blood and a bullet in his neck.

"He was jobbed," I said. "That would take some timing to get conked the same instant you pulled the trigger."

Stan nodded. "An absurdity I pointed out to them. Here's Corey's version."

27

He had been driving up the road to our house when he spotted the gray Plymouth about two hundred feet ahead. He turned off his lights and followed it, staying well behind. When he came around the last big bend near the top of the slope he saw the car parked near the cabin. He took out his gun and walked in from the road, keeping covered, he thought, by the high chaparral. He had never reached the cabin. He had been slugged from behind.

"I believe him," I said. "Did you get a description of the dead man?"

He shook his head. "Is it important? I got his name. The car is his. His name is Jasper Belton."

It didn't ring any bell in me. I asked, "Is Hurst commanding the night watch?"

Stan nodded.

I knew the man; we were semi-friends. I phoned the station, identified myself, and asked, "Is this man Corey is supposed to have killed a big man?"

"Hell, no! Around a hundred and thirty-five pounds. Why do you want to know?"

"Because I think the man who framed Corey is a big man."

"Framed? Come on, Brock!"

"Framed," I repeated. "What about bail for Corey?"

"At this time of night? Do you want to wake up some judge and ask him?"

I hung up without saying good-bye.

"That's a flimsy case they have," I told Stan.

"Maybe not to a jury. Mallory was up there. If they decide to prosecute he will probably be their man." He smiled sadly. "Tom has a very sour view of private detectives. One of them helped his wife get an enormous cash settlement when they were divorced." He rose. "Well, I have to get to bed. We'll talk about it tomorrow, Brock."

I nodded. "Thanks, Stan. If we go to court, you'll be our man. And not at your public defender fee."

"My wife will be happy to hear that," he said.

Stan could have done very well in private practice but he worked for the ACLU. Unlike his private-practice peers, he believed that lawyers should be concerned with justice, not with getting rich. A survey last year showed that lawyers had the highest median income of any profession in the country. Even doctors ranked only fifth.

I had supported the ACLU for a decade, though I was quite often annoyed with the people they defended. Like Bernie, I believe the bad guys should be below the sod or behind bars.

"I hope we can sleep tonight," Jan said.

"I can. I'm bushed. I'm sure the patrols will be going by more often after what happened tonight."

"I've hung a chime on my door knob," Mrs. Casey said, "and I sharpened my knife this morning."

Jan started to chuckle as we were geting undressed.

"What's funny?" I asked.

"Mrs. Casey. God help the poor bastard who tries to open her door. I wish I had her guts."

"She has more room for them. I like your contours better."

I was bushed, but it took a while for me to fall asleep. The way I read the events since the opening incident, I had been the original target for the shadow man. But after he realized the security was too tight at the house, he could have discovered my relationship with Corey and sent me, through him, a warning. *Who is second. . . .*

And the dead Jasper Belton? A stooge? A stooge who realized he was in water too deep for him and planned to get out of town or possibly make a deal with the local police by informing on his partner?

All of this was supposition, none of it facts in evidence. I finally fell asleep. At nine-thirty Jan shook me awake to tell me Bernie was on the phone. I put on a robe and went down.

"I just got a call from McClune," he said. "He told me about Corey being picked up. What's the scoop?"

"It's a long story," I told him. "The gist of it is that Corey was framed."

"McClune tends to agree with that."

"But he doesn't make the decisions. I guess Tom Mallory doesn't agree with McClune, and Mallory is the D.A.'s fair-haired boy."

"Jesus, that's a pair you can draw to! Headline hunters."

"Oh, yes! Do you have a record down there on a man named Jasper Belton?"

"Not here. But McClune and I have sent inquiries to all the jurisdictions in this end of the state."

"Corey will be pleased to hear that. When did you two join his fan club?"

"Don't be a smart-ass, Brock. You know damned well that neither of us would railroad an innocent man."

"I know, Bernie. I apologize. Is there any security guard outfit in town you would recommend?"

"Coastal Guardian. Ask for Joe Hunter. Tell him you know me."

I phoned Coastal Guardian, asked for Joe Hunter, told him my name and address and that I wanted protection from eleven o'clock this morning until I came home for dinner.

"We'll have a man there, Mr. Callahan," he promised. "Now, about our rates—"

"I don't believe there is any need to discuss that," I told him. "My good friend, Lieutenant Vogel, has assured me you are the most competent and inexpensive agency in town."

A silence. "I understand. Thank you."

That should keep their bills within reason, being a friend of eagle-eye, poor-mouth Bernie Vogel.

I told Jan at breakfast about the guard I had ordered and that I would be gone until dinner time.

"Back on the hunt," she said weariliy. "Why didn't I marry a banker or a lawyer?"

30

I said nothing.

The guard was already there when I went out at eleven o'clock, parked in front of the house.

"After you pull out," he explained, "I'll park on your driveway. I can watch both sides of the house and check the other sides from time to time."

The man was a pro. "Sound thinking," I agreed.

McClune was in his outer office when I got there, talking with his secretary. I asked him if bail had been set.

He shook his head. "Not yet. A couple of judges seemed to be inclined to set it, but that pukey Mallory talked them out of it. That man has more clout than he deserves."

"Anything on Belton?"

He shook his head again. "According to his driver's license, he lived in Tritown. He was a young man. He could still have parents living there. The way it usually works with these drifters, the address on their license is a couple of years old and they never stay in one place long enough to change it."

"May I talk with Corey?"

"Of course. Tell the sergeant I gave you permission."

Corey was sitting on the bed in his cell, staring down at the floor. He looked up and managed a smile. "Have you ever been in jail?"

"Not in San Valdesto. I suppose your father is pissed off at me."

He shook his head. "At you, never! At me, yes. He said I should have been more careful. He said you would have been."

"You can tell him I've been bonged on the head a few times."

"But never when you were carrying a gun, I bet."

"No. Mostly on the football field. Is there anything you can tell me that I don't already know?"

He shrugged. "Only what I'm guessing. I think that Belton is just a stooge for that guy asking about you in Los Angeles. I think they were out to get you, but decided you had too much security to take the risk. I think they trapped me into following that car up to the shack so they could frame me and send a message to you."

I stared at him in amazement. He had not only studied under me, he had inherited my instincts. "That is exactly the way I read it," I told him.

"And the way I figure it," he went on, "that Los Angeles creep wants you to think framing me was the end of it, to put you off guard."

"I agree."

"But," he pointed out, "I'm the one who's sitting here. And I'm the one who could wind up in prison—or maybe executed."

I had no immediate answer to that. I asked, "And Belton? Why do you think he was shot?"

"Probably because he decided he was in over his head and figured he could make a deal with the law if he informed on his pal."

"That's the way I see it. Corey, you are not going to wind up in the slammer and you are not going to be executed."

He stared at me. "I'm already in the slammer!"

I had no answer to that one, immediate or otherwise. What could I say? "Keep the faith," I said.

"I'll try. Brock, get that bastard!"

"I will," I promised.

I stopped on the way out to ask McClune if he knew the name of the private investigator who had made Mallory's ex-wife rich.

He nodded. "Barry Fielding. He's a real mean tiger. He works almost as deviously as you do. He calls his office Fielding Investigations. It's on the second floor of the Hollister Building."

The Hollister Building was one of the town's oldest office buildings, but well kept up. Barry's office was at the end of the hall.

The lettering on the opaque glass of his door read *Walk In*. So I walked in.

McClune's description of him as a tiger had led me to imagine he would be one of those old-time pulp-style mugs, big and mean and wearing a cheap suit.

A short, slim man in a Brooks Brothers type of suit and button-down collar on his oxford shirt was standing near the window, checking his file cabinet. He was wearing horn-rimmed glasses and a quiet tie.

"Mr. Fielding?" I asked.

He nodded.

"My name is Brock Callahan," I said, "and—"

"*The* Brock Callahan?" he asked.

"The only one I know. Have you heard of me?"

"Have I ever! Those guys in L.A. are still talking about you. They made you sound like Superman. I just moved up here a year ago. How can I serve you?"

"Well," I said, "it might be a violation of your client relationship. It's about Tom Mallory."

"That son of a bitch? He tried to get the state to take away my license. Why do you want to know about him?"

I told him about Corey being incarcerated and why and my belief that he was being jobbed and that I felt Mallory was scalp-hunting.

"I know Corey," he said. "Good kid. What do you want from me?"

"Something I can use to help him, at least get him some extra time on a continuance. I suppose that's unethical."

"How else would we survive?" he asked. "Could I take you to lunch?"

"Nope. Lunch is on me. Your choice of restaurants."

"Plotkin's Pantry?"

"Perfect."

Over corned-beef sandwiches on dark rye bread with kosher pickles and draft Einlicher at Plotkin's he told me about his leverage in the Mallory divorce trial.

"I suppose you know," he said, "what a Moral Majority addict the D.A. is."

"I do."

"Well, licentious Tom would be in deep trouble if his boss ever learned his history. That was my leverage in the case. Tom has some really kinky sexual appetites. The only place in town that caters to those customers is the Arden Massage Parlor on lower Main Street. I interviewed several of the girls, including one of them who was quitting and agreed to testify if we needed her. We didn't need her. I gave the names of the girls to Mrs. Mallory and let her tell Tom what she had learned. It was a breeze after that."

"That's kind of doubtful investigative ethics, Barry."

He smiled. "The pot is talking about the kettle. I got the word on you in L.A."

"Those bums lie a lot," I explained. "Do you have any names I could use?"

"So you could blackmail Tom? That's doubtful investigative ethics, Brock."

"Except," I said cooly, "I am trying to keep a nice kid out of jail and you were trying to make your client rich."

"True." He smiled again. "I thought I was the master of moral rationalization. I should have studied under you."

"The names—please?"

"I'll give you only their first names, Lois, Yvette, and Joan."

"Thank you."

"Any time, Brock. And if Corey gets sentenced and you need a partner—?"

"You'll be my first choice," I lied.

34

CHAPTER 5

TOM MALLORY IS A BIG, BLUFF IRISHMAN who probably belongs to every service club in town. He was talking into a dictating machine when I entered his office.

He turned off the machine and glared at me. "I suppose you're here to beg for your junior partner."

"He's not my partner," I said, "and I'm not here to beg. I hoped we could talk sensibly."

"Talk," he said. "I'll decide if it's sensible."

"I'm not sure if you know about the events leading up to last night's murder."

"I do. Your buddy, McClune, filled me in. Jesus, Callahan, if you were the prosecutor and you had a case as strong as this one, what would you do? The kid's there with the gun that killed Belton. He has a bump on his head and Belton has a rock in his hand."

"I would remember what McClune had told me and I would weigh all the evidence. I wouldn't go rushing into court with a case this flawed. It reeks of frame-up."

"Maybe to you. And what's this about a mystery man McClune mentioned?"

"I have a theory that the man who killed Belton was really after me. Belton was only his stooge."

He shook his head. He smiled. "Don't tell me that's No-

35

wicki's defense! A theory? The trial shouldn't last long. Has the man got a name?"

"Every man has a name. I don't happen to know it, but I'm determined to get it."

"Get it," he said, "before you come back here."

"As you wish," I said. "Give my best to Lois, Yvette, and Joan."

He turned rigid. "You bastard! You've been talking to Fielding."

"Fielding who? I don't know anybody named Fielding."

"Blackmail," he said hoarsely. "I wish I'd left the machine on."

"Turn it on. I'll repeat it."

"You bastard!" he said again.

I said quietly, "I'm doing you a favor, Tom. I'm preventing you from making a damned fool of yourself. All I'm asking for is time. I'm not even asking for bail. But when the trial date is set, I wish you'd agree to a continuance."

He took a deep breath and stared past me.

"I might not need it," I pointed out. "But if I do, I want it."

"You've got it," he finally said. "Now get out of here."

I went out with the uncomfortable feeling that I had reverted to my Los Angeles days, when I could not afford the finer points of ethics. Only the rich can afford to be completely honest. Why aren't they?

I drove past our house on the way up the hill to the scene of the crime. Mrs. Casey was out in front, talking to the guard, probably trying to inveigle him into a quick game of gin rummy.

Up, up, up, almost to the crest. It was not only a deserted cabin, it was decrepit—the roof half gone, no glass in its single window. The shadow man and his young stooge could not have stayed here; the cruising deputies would have spotted the Plymouth before last night.

It was not a coincidence that it was on our road. It had

36

been the terminal of a trap; they had watched Corey drive up our road for two nights. They had lured him here and framed him and the shadow man's partner had been the other victim.

I parked on the graveled edge and threaded through the open spaces between the clumps of chaparral. There was no path to the shack still in evidence.

The door was open, hanging on one hinge. It was a shack, no more. No water, no toilet, one room with a packed earth floor, littered with beer cans, bottles, dusty trash, and yellowed newspapers.

Two bright spots stood out on the dusty trash, an empty paper book of matches and a crumpled cigarette package.

Denny's Tavern was imprinted on the matchbook. I knew the place, a workingmen's bar on the Venice-Santa Monica border. Corinth was the cigarette brand, a brand unfamiliar to me.

I heard a "meow" and looked over to see a mangy black cat studying me doubtfully from the doorway. It came in as I went out.

At the sheriff's station I gave McClune the matchbook and the cigarette package. "They were the only clean things in the place," I explained. "They must have been left there recently. I thought you might find some prints on one of them."

"What place?"

"The shack where Corey was framed. Did you phone to Tritown?"

He nodded. "Both of Belton's parents have moved to Arizona. And he hasn't been there for over a year."

"I know where Denny's Tavern is," I told him. "It's on the border of Santa Monica. What about those cigarettes? Have you ever heard of them?"

He shook his head.

"A clue, maybe?"

"Maybe. That was sloppy of us. We should have gone

over the place more carefully." He shook his head. "Rookies!"

"They'll learn. And you've always got me. Stick it to Bernie Saturday night."

"Huh! I should be so lucky. He told me he's inviting a guy named Larry Rubin. Do you know him?"

"Yup. I knew him in Los Angeles. He's like you—he draws to inside straights and three-card flushes."

"Go!" he said.

I went home.

I told the guard I would need protection again tomorrow, from nine-thirty in the morning until I came home.

"I hope the boss assigns me," he said. "I like the clean air up here and the great chow."

"The chow?"

"Right. That housekeeper of yours made me a great afternoon snack. Is she married?"

"Widowed," I said. "Are you single?"

"No, damn it!"

Jan was in the den watching the tube when I came in. "They caught the Valley Intruder," she said.

The broad face of the Los Angeles sheriff was on the tube, explaining how it had happened; citizens had made the capture.

Forty Los Angeles detectives had been working on the case for a month, assisted by the county sheriff's department. Even the San Francisco police had been brought into the hunt when the Intruder had killed a man up there and raped his wife.

The Intruder had made the mistake of wandering into a Chicano neighborhood. He had tried to drag a woman from her car so he could steal it. Her husband had knocked him loose with a crowbar. A crowd had gathered and were slowly beating him to death when the police arrived. At the end, according to the sheriff, the man had been begging for police protection.

"Those damned dumb cops!" Jan said. "Couldn't they have pretended they had a flat tire and got there too late to save him?"

"Easy, sister."

"Easy, hell! Now they'll have an eighteen-month, two-million-dollar trial and some smart-ass lawyer will get him assigned to a mental institution and when they think he's sane again they'll put him back on the street so he can continue his career."

"I think it's time for a drink," I said.

"Make them strong," she said. "Scotch and soda for me."

She sipped her Scotch and soda, I my Bourbon over ice. "Learn anything today?" she asked.

"Not much. I talked Tom Mallory out of rushing into court to convict Corey. I convinced him he could look bad if and when the real killer is found. What have you been doing?"

"Fretting and fuming, mostly. But then I got to think-ing—we're lucky, aren't we, Brock?"

"At the most conservative estimate we are probably luck-ier than ninety percent of the people on this planet. At the moment, we are a lot luckier than Corey Raleigh."

"Yes. We must learn to count our blessings."

"That's old-fashioned. This is the me, me, me genera-tion."

"But not tonight," she said. "Tonight we will be the we generation, you and me."

At dinner, Mrs. Casey said, "That's a real nice man who was guarding the house today. I took a snack out to him around three o'clock."

I nodded. "He told me."

"I wonder if he's married," she said.

"He is."

She looked crestfallen. I said, "But he's not happy about it. And he told me he wants to come back tomorrow just for the clean air and the fine food."

"If he comes back," she said stiffly, "he can enjoy the clean air."

Another romance nipped in the bud. Mrs. Casey would *never* marry a divorced man.

We didn't sit up for the news that night. I locked all the doors and windows and we went to bed for our incursion into the we generation.

The morning dawned hot and clear. It would be hotter in the lower Main Street area where I intended to investigate the tawdry bars and cheap hotels. It seemed logical for me to assume the shadow man would not be staying at the Biltmore.

Yesterday's guard was not back today. They had sent a younger, thinner man, too young to arouse any emotion in Mrs. Casey except the maternal. For that emotion, she has her Corey.

There was a for-sale sign on the Crider lawn. It would not be there long; in Montevista, homes for sale are not that blatantly advertised. They are handled much more discreetly by the brokers' multiple-listing requirement.

Back to the mean streets. . . . I ran the gamut of bars from A to Z, from The Alamo Café to Ziggy's Hangout. I was welcomed in the places where I was known, suspicioned in the others, informed in none. That used up the morning.

I had a bottle of Beck's dark and a steak sandwich at Joe's Grille and made the hotel run in the afternoon. From the seediest to the almost respectable I traveled, learning nothing until I came to my last, best hope—the Travis Hotel.

I had two informants there and a black and friendly day clerk.

The clerk said, "A big bald man with a long scar on his cheek?" He nodded. "He checked out yesterday."

"What was his name?"

His smile was cynical. "The most common name on our register—John Smith."

"Damn it! If he comes back, you'll alert me, won't you?"

"I sure will."

I asked him if either of my informants was in his room.

"Not today," he said. "They're both in the drunk tank. I'm sure they didn't have any contact with the man you're looking for."

I thanked him and put a ten-dollar bill on the counter. I drove to the station and Bernie was there. I told him what I had learned at the hotel.

He told me, "We had an officer there yesterday, about twenty minutes after Baldy left." He reached into a drawer and took out an empty cigarette package. "The maid hadn't cleaned the room yet, but this was all we found. With no prints on it."

It was a Corinth package.

I said, "That's the same brand I found in that shack where Belton was murdered. That should prove to Mallory that his case isn't as strong as he thinks it is."

He shook his head. "Not to a jury. It proves nothing."

"Have *you* ever heard of that brand before?"

He sighed. "Brock, I am sure there are a thousand brands of cigarettes I have never heard of."

I said nothing.

"Cheer up," he said. "At least the heat's off you. The man has left town."

"Maybe. But even if he has, he'll be back. It wasn't Corey he was after, not originally."

"Your instinct again?"

I nodded. "What else do I have?"

"Muscle," he said. "And now I must get back to work. I'm two days behind in my reports."

On the way to the freeway I stopped in at Nowicki's office. He wasn't there. The volunteer secretary in the office told me he was in a conference with Tom Mallory and Chief Chandler Harris at the courthouse. They were spiritual twins, Mallory a head hunter, Harris a headline hunter. It

41

was a county kill; what interest could Harris have in it? Publicity was my guess.

Jan, Mrs. Casey told me when I came home, had gone out to visit a former client and possible future client in Slope Ranch. "I tried to talk her out of it," Mrs. Casey added, "but she said she was going stir crazy."

"Aren't *you*?" I asked.

She shook her head. "I want that freak to find me. Anybody who would try to frame sweet Corey is on my enemy list."

"Why don't we have a smidgin of good Irish whiskey while Jan is gone?"

She nodded. "We're the sly ones, aren't we?"

We sat out in back and discussed the capture of the Valley Intruder. "You notice those Chicanos didn't run and hide," she pointed out. "They're a lot like the Irish, aren't they?"

I nodded. "And good Catholics, too."

She gave me a baleful look.

"No comment, please," I said. "I still have a lot of Catholic in me."

"No comment," she said. "Let's talk about the Dodgers."

CHAPTER 6

I STARTED TO GET NERVOUS AT FIVE O'CLOCK. Slope Ranch is on the other end of town from Montevista, but not so far away that Jan shouldn't be home by five. Mrs. Casey had told me she had left right after lunch.

She came home at five-thirty, carrying packages. "As long as I was out of the house," she explained, "I thought it might be a good time to get in some shopping. And Mrs. Casey will have to go to the grocery store tomorrow."

"I'll take her."

"Is that our new regime? Are we going to be perpetual hermits?"

"Please, Jan—!" I said. "We're *all* uptight!"

"I know," she said quietly. "I'm sorry. There's nothing you can do about it."

Nowicki phoned after dinner to tell me that his conference with Harris and Mallory had gone well. "Mallory," he said, "was almost reasonable, for a change. Do you think he's got religion?"

"No! How did Harris worm his way into the act?"

"Because one of his officers learned that the man Vogel told him about, the man who asked about you in Los Angeles, was in a city hotel. You've finally done Harris a favor. He can get some ink out of the murder. Now that the Valley Intruder has been caught, this case could be headline news."

43

"But Mallory wouldn't believe the man who asked about me was involved."

"Until now—when they realized the two of them can get some ink out of it. This could be the new Valley Intruder and that cat gimmick should go over big on the idiot box."

"Oh, yes," I sadly agreed.

There is nothing you can do about it, Jan had said. That canny bastard was relying on that. There had to be something I could do about it.

I loaded the old Colt before we went to bed that night and put it back on the shelf in the closet.

"Wouldn't it be safer to have a guard outside?" Jan asked.

"Don't worry. We'll be safe."

She studied me. "You want him to come in, don't you? You and Mrs. Casey want him to come in."

"Of course not!" I lied.

The for-sale sign was no longer on the Crider lawn when Mrs. Casey and I went grocery shopping next morning, but the agent I knew was taking a couple into the house. He had a key.

"I bet they left," Mrs. Casey said. "The sissies!"

"Maybe," I suggested, "they're living it up at the Biltmore."

She made no comment.

Mrs. Casey is a dedicated comparison shopper; it was eleven o'clock when we loaded the car.

She had bought some grapes and Brie cheese to take to Corey. "You know how he loves them both," she said. "You won't mind driving me there, will you?"

"I'll be glad to drive you there," I told here, "but I'm not sure what their rules are about feeding a prisoner."

"Let me handle that part," she said.

McClune was there—and cooperative. Corey was reading a tattered paperback reprint of *The Maltese Falcon,* quite possibly for the twentieth time.

He was looking less gloomy today. He told us, "Nowicki

44

was here this morning. He thinks there's a possibility now that I might get out on bail. But it would take more money than I can raise."

"If it happens," I said, "I'll pay for the bond. You can work it off by guarding the house again."

"He could even stay with us," Mrs. Casey suggested. "I'm sure he wouldn't charge as much as those guards you hired. And he'd be getting his meals free."

That should run up our grocery bill. Mrs. Casey goes gourmet when Corey is eating with us.

The mailman came right after lunch and I went out to get it. Our only first-class mail was a postcard, another seven-word message. It read: "You can't hide forever. I'll be back." It was postmarked from Los Angeles.

"Any interesting mail?" Jan asked.

"Just the garbage mail," I told her. "I have to take a short trip this afternoon, but I'll be home before dinner."

"Trip to where?"

"To Tritown."

"What's in Tritown?"

"A former cop friend," I lied. "He could have some information I need."

I put the card in an envelope and took it with me to the sheriff's station. McClune was out for lunch; I gave it to the fingerprint man.

It had occurred to me this morning while I was waiting for Mrs. Casey that though Jasper Belton's parents had moved to Arizona, he could still have friends in town. Through the gray parched hills I drove for fifteen miles and then down the long winding road that led into the verdant green of Avocado Valley.

It is a town of about three thousand inhabitants, many of them retired farm families. There were cars on the high-school parking lot; they obviously had a summer session.

45

The principal was in his outer office, a thin gray-haired man in blue slacks and a blue-and-white-striped golf shirt.

I told him I had come from San Valdesto to get what information he might have on Jasper Belton.

"Are you a police officer?"

I shook my head. "I'm retired now. But I work with the police in town occasionally. Sort of a—oh, community service."

Jasper, he told me, had been a puzzle to him, a lad who had the capability of being an honor student but maintained a running dispute with all of his teachers.

"He seemed determined to become our leading anti-establishment student. He reveled in controversy. And the rowdies he hung around with encouraged him. He was the only bright boy in the group." He shook his head. "What a waste!"

"Does he have any relatives in town?"

"A stepsister. But I would suggest you don't question her. She is furious about the fact that Mr. Belton didn't phone her from Arizona to tell her about—about what happened, not until two days later."

"It's possible," I explained, "that the police hadn't located his parents before then. My mission is to find Jasper's murderer."

"I see." He frowned. "I don't know what to advise you to do. If you want, I'll phone her and explain the situation."

"I'd appreciate it."

I didn't hear the conversation; he phoned from his inner office. When he came out, he was smiling. "You were right. Mr. Belton phoned her this morning and explained the police delay." He handed me a card. "Here is her name and address."

Mrs. James Patino lived at 425 Orchard Lane. He gave me the directions to the house.

It was a small two-story white frame house with a house-wide screened front porch, right out of the Midwest corn belt.

46

A short, slim blonde girl wearing faded jeans and a T-shirt was waiting for me on the porch. She asked, "Are you the officer from San Valdesto?"

I nodded.

"I only have an hour before leaving for Arizona," she said. "My husand is coming home from work to drive me to the Temple airport."

"I'll be brief. I have two reasons to want to find the man who killed Jasper. First of all, he meant to get me. Second, when he decided he couldn't, he framed a young friend of mine. I have reason to believe the man who killed Jasper pretended to be his friend. He is the same man who threatened me."

"I wish I could help," she said, "but I don't know any of Jasper's new friends. I haven't even heard from him since he ran away from Arcadia House."

Arcadia House was a mental institution in the San Fernando Valley. I didn't ask her the reason for his being there. I asked, "Did he write to you when he was there?"

"Rarely," she said. "And he never mentioned any friends." She took a breath. "I hope you find that so-called friend of his."

"So do I, Mrs. Patino. I hope I find him before he finds me. I apologize for intruding at this time."

"I'm glad you did," she said.

Back up the long winding road out of the green valley to the parched hills. Scarface the intimidator, I reasoned, could well have spent some time in a mental hospital. Could that be his connection to Belton? There was a way to find out.

I told the guard in front of the house that I would need round-the-clock service tomorrow. He assured me it would be supplied.

In the house, Jan asked, "Did your cop friend have any information that will help?"

"A doubtful lead," I told her, "but I have to check it out. I'm going down to Los Angeles tomorrow. I told the man outside we want twenty-four-hour service until I come home."

"It's time for a drink," she said. "If this keeps up we could turn into drunkards."

I kissed her. "Easy, honey. One day at a time."

"For how long?"

I didn't answer.

"Damn me!" she said. "I'm becoming a shrew!"

I didn't argue with her.

The original note had a San Valdesto postmark, today's card a Los Angeles postmark. The alert from Heinie had come from Los Angeles; that had to be the man's stamping ground. He probably had left here when he sensed, or was told, that the noose was tightening. He had left town twenty minutes before the officer searched his hotel room. Did he, I wondered, have another ally in town?

McClune phoned before dinner to tell me they had not been able to raise any usable prints on the postcard, not even with the laser.

"How about Corey?" I asked him. "Nowicki told me this morning that it was possible he might be granted bail."

"That could take some time," he said. "I can imagine that both Mallory and Harris are carefully weighing the public relations advantage on both sides of that decision."

I told him what I had learned in Tritown and that I planned to visit Arcadia House tomorrow.

"Good work, tiger," he said. "Luck."

It was not only my ill-gotten wealth that had done it; it was probable that I would have enjoyed much better police cooperation in my Los Angeles days if I had known some high-ranking police officers who played poker.

Another troubled night; my stomach rumbled and my bad knee ached. From the freeway came the sound of the diesel trucks, from the sky the distant drone of a plane coming into the San Valdesto airport.

The local radio informed us in the morning that there had

48

been another juvenile assault on the roadside mailboxes in Slope Ranch. One youth was being held. He was not an invader from lower Main Street; he was a Slope Rancher who had rammed a steel mailbox post with his Porsche.

Jan got up from the table and turned off the set. "Why?" she asked. "What could they be angry about?"

I shrugged. "Maybe boredom?"

"Or maybe drugs?"

"That's a better guess," I agreed. "If their parents won't give them the money for dope they have to steal it. That's what is happening up here. So we get the daytime burglars."

"Thank God, we don't have kids!" Jan said.

I didn't agree. I kept my mouth shut.

CHAPTER 7

TRAFFIC WAS LIGHT ON THE FREEWAY UNTIL I reached Ventura. It grew heavier and slower all the way to Tarzana. I turned off there; Arcadia House is in Tarzana. The street traffic was less clogged.

The parking lot was about half full when I got there. The patients' building was large and two stories tall; the administration building small, only one story, connected by a passageway with the larger building. All of it was white stucco, trimmed in varnished redwood.

The office of Dial Forest, Administrator, was directly across the lobby from the entrance. In the outer office, a heavyset woman in a blue knit dress was busily typing at her desk near the counter when I entered.

She looked up and smiled at me.

I told her my name and said, "I'm working with the police in San Valdesto on the murder of a former patient of yours, a young man named Jasper Belton. I came here for what information you might have on him."

"The name isn't familiar to me," she said, "but I've only been here for three months. One moment, please."

She went into the inner office and came out in a few minutes. "Mr. Forest will see you," she said.

Dial Forest was a handsome young man in a conservative

gray three-piece suit, either a yuppie or a transplanted east-
erner. He didn't rise as I entered; he was riffling through a
stack of file cards on his desk.

"Ah, yes," he said finally, "here it is, Jasper Belton. He
was discharged—" He paused. "He left here six months
ago."

"His stepsister told me he ran away."

He shook his head. "He came of his own volition and left
the same way. We had no authority to hold him."

"What was his problem—drugs?"

"We don't release the medical records of our patients, Mr.
Callahan."

"Why not? They can't hurt him now. He's dead. He was
murdered."

He stared at me. "My secretary didn't tell me that!" He
looked at the card again. "He was suffering from schizophrenia. As I remember, he seemed to be improving when he
left."

"Do you have the address he gave you when he was admitted?"

He nodded. "Four-twenty-five Orchard Lane. That's in
Tritown, a small town in Avocado Valley."

"I know. I was there."

He frowned. "Wait—I remember now! I saw him about a
month later. He was working as a bag boy in a Santa
Monica supermarket. I never saw him after that and we buy
all our groceries there. It's a Von's chain store."

That would be a dead end by now. I asked, "Do you remember any of your patients he was close to when he was
here?"

He shook his head. "I'm sure there were none. He was
extremely reclusive."

"I'm thinking particularly of a heavy bald man with a
long scar on his right cheek."

He shook his head again. "I would have remembered a
man like that."

51

It suddenly occurred to me that Dial Forest went a long way through heavy traffic to buy his groceries. I mentioned this.

He sighed. "I live with my mother and she refuses to leave Santa Monica. I, sir, am a fourth-generation Santa Monican."

I thanked him and left and headed for his home town.

Denny's Tavern is in Venice, about half a block from the Santa Monica border. It is an old brick building of three floors, the two above the tavern inhabited by Denny and his wife. The last time I was here there had also been three teenagers in the family group, but they must have flown the coop by now.

Denny had been a jockey at one time, but he rarely finished in the money. Two stout construction workers in hard hats were at the bar when I entered, quaffing beer. A thin, middle-aged woman in khaki shorts and halter was studying *The Racing Form* at a corner table and working a pocket calculator.

Denny had put on weight. He studied me, frowning. "I know you," he said. "But from where?"

I started to answer, but he held up a hand. "Callahan! The Rock! Where the hell have you been?"

"I live in San Valdesto now. I'm more or less retired."

"You must have retired rich. Ain't that the town that won't let in Democrats?"

"We have a couple of them."

"You drink Beck's dark, right?"

"When I can't get Einlicher."

He set a bottle and a glass in front of me and said, "On the house. What brings you down to God's country?"

"I'm looking for a man, a big man. He's bald and he has a long scar on his right cheek."

"I had a guy like that come here for his cigarettes, but I never learned his name. He hardly ever bought a drink."

"Corinth cigarettes?"

He nodded. "This was the only place in town he could buy 'em. I got on to them when the missus and I went to Greece. They're made there. I still smoke 'em but I don't have many buyers. I guess your friend must have found some other store that sells them. He hasn't been here for a month."

"He's not a friend of mine. Do you know a young man named Jasper Belton?"

"Hell, yes! He worked for me for a couple of months. He mopped the place out—you know—the peon labor. What about him?"

"He was murdered in San Valdesto. Don't you read the papers?"

"Only the sports pages. My stomach is too weak for the rest of it. What's going on, Brock? You said you were retired."

"This one is personal. Scarface threatened me and then framed a young friend of mine for Belton's murder."

"He threatened *you?* Has he got a death wish, or what?"

"He threatened me by mail. Was Belton working here when he was coming in for cigarettes?"

"He was. Hey, wait—you think this big slob killed Jasper?"

I nodded.

"Jesus! I'd better keep my forty-five handy. What's his beef with you?"

"I can only guess. My best guess is that he must have been some hoodlum I had put away when I was working here."

The woman in shorts and halter came from the table, put a slip and some money on the bar and said, "Remember now, Denny, I've got a copy of those."

"I know, Grace! You've told me that a hundred times!"

She smiled and left, taking her calculator along.

"Horse players," Denny said. "They're bad enough. But women!"

I didn't comment. I wrote my phone number on a paper napkin and handed it to him. "If Scarface shows up, call me in San Valdesto. If I'm not there, give my wife the message. I'll be phoning her." I put a ten-dollar bill on the counter. "That should pay for the call."

He pushed the bill back. "Make it my contribution to the hunt. This slob shapes up as a public menace."

I thought of that silly game called treasure hunt we had played in high school, leaving clues at every hidden stop. Was that what the man was playing with me?

He had lured Corey to the shack by sending Jasper up the hill in the Plymouth. He had left clues there that had sent me to Arcadia House and Denny's Tavern. Why? To get me out of town, to make me an unprotected target? Or was somebody else slated to be his second victim?

I drove to Heinie's.

He was behind the bar, arguing with a customer, as usual. "You!" he said. "It's about time! What brings you into my humble establishment?"

"Your gourmet cuisine," I said. "I'll have a steak sandwich and beaker of Einlicher."

"Yes, sir. Coming right up, sir."

He went to the kitchen; I went to a corner booth. When he came out of the kitchen, he poured a beaker of Einlicher and brought it to the booth. José, his lackey of all trades, took over behind the bar.

Heinie slid into the booth across from me. "I've been reading about what's happening in your town. Trouble, buddy?"

I nodded. "Trouble."

"Who's this Corey Raleigh I've been reading about?"

"A young man I trained, a private investigator. The way it's shaping up, that man who asked about me in here could have framed him."

"How'd he find you? He didn't get your address from me."

"I don't know. When I find him, I'll know."

"If you find him. Do you know his name?"

I shook my head.

"God damn it, I should have asked him!" Heinie said.

"Don't feel guilty. He would have lied."

The lunch trade was beginning to come in now, filling the booths. The drinking trade was lining up at the bar. Heinie said, "I've got to get to work. Hang around after you've eaten, okay?"

I nodded. "I've run out of places to go."

Heinie was still busy when I had finished eating. I went into his small office and made a collect call to the house.

Jan answered. I told her I might be home today or might stay over; I wasn't sure yet.

She said, "A man named Harley Belton phoned about half an hour ago. He's staying at the Sheraton here. He left the room and phone number and wants you to call him. Could that be the boy's father?"

"Probably."

She gave me the numbers and said, "Now, damn you, *please* be careful!"

"I will. I'll phone you again some time today."

I phoned the Sheraton and Harley Belton was in. I identified myself.

He said, "I'm Jasper Belton's father. Sheriff McClune gave me your name. Where are you now?"

"In Los Angeles. In a bar near Beverly Hills. I should be home tonight."

"Stay there," he said. "That's where it all started. I want to help you find that bastard."

"Mr. Belton, that could be extremely dangerous."

"Don't tell me about danger, Mr. Callahan. I spent thirty years in the Marine Corps. Wait for me!"

He sounded like my kind of man. I gave him the address and directions on how to get here.

The lunch trade began to drift out; the bar trade stayed to argue. Heinie came over to sit across from me, bringing his

55

steak sandwich and Einlicher with him. José followed him, bringing me another beaker. We didn't talk much.

I spotted Harley Belton as soon as he walked in. He could have been the model for a Marine poster, lean as a greyhound, ramrod-straight shoulders, eyes of arctic blue, and a crew haircut.

He walked right to the booth where I was reading the morning *Times*. "You're Callahan, aren't you? I've watched you play."

"Guilty. Can I buy you a drink?"

"A double bourbon on the rocks," he said. He sat down across from me.

I called out the order to Heinie and asked, "Have you had lunch?"

He nodded. "I brought a couple of sandwiches along to eat on the way. Have you learned anything here?"

I told him what I had learned and my suspicion that our quarry evidently wanted to play hide-and-seek. I told him about the clues he had left behind and the ploy he had used to trap Corey.

"Those cuties can outfox themselves," he said. "I brought along the letters from my son. There might be some leads in them."

I said, "Mrs. Patino told me he rarely wrote to her."

"She's my wife's daughter," he explained. "She and Jasper were never very close. My first wife died three years after he was born. I can't say I was much of a father, away on duty so often, and Jasper never really got along with my present wife."

I said nothing.

He took a swallow of his drink. "Gad, that was a dumb move to Arizona! I thought Tritown was boring. Compared with Sun City, it's Paris."

"How old are you?"

"Fifty-three. I joined the Marines when I was eighteen

and retired when I was forty-eight. I had a smart buddy in the service who told me where to invest my money, so I'm not hurting. Could I buy you a drink? I'm going to have another."

He had another double bourbon, I another beer.

"You got any kids?" he asked.

I shook my head. "I married too late."

He took a deep breath. "I had one—and blew it! He was a smart and sensitive kid. It's not easy for a dumb Marine to understand a smart kid."

Again, I said nothing.

"And killing the creep," he said, "won't bring Jasper back."

"Easy, Harley! We're not the law."

"I know, I know," he said wearily. "Jasper—that's a dumb name to give a kid, right? My first wife had a rich uncle by that name. Hell, he didn't leave the kid a dime." He finished his drink. "Santa Monica and Venice, that's where most of his letters were written. Should we headquarter there?"

"It makes sense. I know a fairly nice motel in Santa Monica that won't gouge us. You can follow me."

He followed me. He practically tailgated me to the Bayside Inn. He was driving a new Camaro, but with a lot more horses under the hood than Corey's old one. Harley, like Larry and Bernie, didn't favor foreign products, probably their only area of agreement.

At the desk, the dapper clerk smirked and said, "Twin beds or a double bed, gentlemen?"

Harley turned rigid. I said quickly, "Twin beds," thus saving the man from a flying trip through the plate-glass window that fronted on the parking lot.

In our second-floor room, Harley said, "This is really kook country, isn't it?"

"It is," I agreed. "Let's look over the letters."

57

"The name of the man we want isn't in them," he told me. "They were mostly about the kids he met here. The only man he mentioned is somebody the kids called Big Bear."

"Why don't you make out a list of them," I suggested, "while I take a shower?"

He nodded agreement.

CHAPTER 8

HARLEY HAD THE LIST MADE OUT WHEN I came from the shower. Some were only first names. But there were other means of identification; one a poet, another a guitar player, another the publisher of an antiestablishment press in Venice.

Harley smiled. "Names, names— Guess what my middle name is."

"You tell me."

"I'll give you a hint. I grew up in Milwaukee."

"Davidson?"

He nodded. "My old man grew up with Bill Harley and Walter Davidson. The difference is that they built motorcycles and he only rode them. So they wound up rich and he wound up with a couple of broken legs."

"And you wound up in the Marines. Do you have any tattoos?"

"None I'm going to show you. A tattoo is also a call sounded before taps, notifying us to go to quarters."

"I'm sure there's some symbolism there that escapes me," I said. "To get back to the here and now, what did Jasper say about this man called Big Bear?"

He picked up one of the letters and read aloud: "'I first saw him when I was working in a Venice bar. He never

59

talked much there. Later I got to know him at several of Duane's parties. Duane admires him, a true revolutionary, he claims. I'm not sure I agree but he certainly is interesting.'"

"That's the only time Jasper mentioned him?"

He nodded. "That was his last letter to me."

"This Duane is the one who publishes the *Venice Vendetta,* isn't he?"

He nodded again.

"We've got a lot of time before dinner," I suggested. "Let's run over and talk with Duane."

He tapped the letter. "This is Jasper's last address. Let's go there first."

It was an ancient frame house of two stories, newly painted, only a few blocks from Denny's Tavern. The sign next to the door informed us that there was a room for rent. Harley turned the old-fashioned bell crank in the door.

A normally thin but currently pregnant black woman in a flowered print caftan opened the door a few moments later.

Harley said, "I am Jasper Belton's father. My friend, here, is a police officer from San Valdesto. Could we ask you some questions?"

"Of course," she said. "Come in."

She led us to a small and sparsely furnished room in the front of the house. It now served as a living room but had probably been a front parlor when the house was built.

We sat on a worn velour-covered couch, she in a matching chair. She said, "Your son was a fine boy, Mr. Belton. I liked him."

"Yes," he said. "And I'm afraid I was a bad father. Do you know any of his friends—particularly a man who calls himself Big Bear?"

She shook her head. "Jasper's friends rarely came here. He knew I didn't like them. Jasper mentioned that man but I never learned his real name."

"Was he moody when he was here?"

60

"At times," she said. "Who isn't—at times? He told me that doctor up in the San Fernando Valley thought he had schizophrenia." Her smile was sad. "You know what Jasper told *him?* He told him 'physician, heal thyself.' Doctors—! I'll be going to a midwife."

"Was he ever on drugs when he was here?"

She hesitated.

"I have to know," Harley said.

She nodded. "He was, I'm almost sure, the last week he was here. Before that, if he was, it didn't show."

"Nothing else?"

"Nothing," she said, "except that I sure miss him." Tears came to her eyes. "I hope you find that mother-fucking son of a bitch!"

"I assure you, ma'am," Harley said in an even voice, "that we intend to find the man you have just described so accurately."

He was silent as we walked to my car. After I had started the engine, he said, "Nice lady. I should have married *her.*"

"Duane next?" I asked.

He nodded.

The office of the *Venice Vendetta* was a narrow place, sandwiched between a deserted sidewalk restaurant and an adult bookstore.

A thin youth with a pale complexion and wheat-colored hair was laying out photos on a table on the other side of the counter. He was wearing a pair of old khaki trousers, sandals, and a sweat-stained T-shirt.

He studied us. "Yes—?"

"I'm Jasper Belton's father," Harley said. "You're Duane?"

"Yeah. So? And who's your friend?"

"I have a number of names," I said. "You can call me trouble."

"Oh, God!" he said. "A comedian!"

"And large. We came here to find out the name of the

61

man known locally as Big Bear. We think he's the man who murdered your friend Jasper."

"Jasper—dead?" He came to the counter.

"Dead," I said. "Don't you read the papers?"

"Not the commercial ones. Jesus!"

"All we want from you," I told him, "is the name of the man who calls himself Big Bear."

"So help me, I don't know it. I never knew it."

Harley said, "Jasper told me in one of his letters that you admired the man."

He nodded. "Oh, yes! Until the bastard left town owing me seventy dollars."

I smiled. "I guess he wasn't the true revolutionary you thought he was."

He glared at me. "God damn you, lay off! Jasper was my friend."

"So was the man who killed him," I said. "The man he met through you. Learn to live with that!"

"You said you *think* he killed him," he pointed out. "You don't *know*. I have no reason to want to defend him after he stiffed me. But a man is innocent until he is proven guilty."

"Yes. Is Big Bear bald? Does he have a scar on his right cheek?"

He stared at me and nodded.

"Does he smoke Corinth cigarettes?"

He nodded again.

"Do you know where he buys them now? He stopped buying them at Denny's Tavern."

He shook his head. "I don't know where he bought them, then or later."

Harley put the list of names on the counter. "Could you help us with the last names and addresses of these friends of Jasper's? They might have some information we can use."

He read the list. "I can do that. All of them are subscribers to my paper."

It was still too early for dinner when we came back to the

62

motel. Harley went in to take a shower. I read through the addresses Duane had given us and then phoned Jan.

"You won't be home tonight," she guessed.

"I won't. Anything new up there?"

"Nothing. And with you?"

"Belton and I are working together. He's a good man to have along, a retired Marine."

"That should make him your kind of man. I miss you, Brock."

"It's mutual. And you be careful! We can't be sure that man is still in town here."

"I'm well protected, sweetie. Mrs. Casey is now sleeping in our bedroom and she brought her dagger along."

Harley came in as I hung up.

"The missus?" he asked.

I nodded.

"You happily married?"

"Most of the time. Are you?"

"Not lately," he said. "You think maybe I'm trying to transfer my sense of guilt to my wife?"

I shrugged. "That's too complicated for me."

"Yeh. You know, you and I are a lot alike."

I grinned at him. "Maybe we should have asked for a double bed."

"Let's get off that kick, Brock." He paused. "We're going to find that bastard, aren't we?"

"Or die trying. Did you see much action in the Marines?"

"I killed a few people." He took a deep breath. "If you don't mind, I'd rather not talk about it. Should we eat here?"

"We may as well. The food's not bad and they have a liquor license."

He had his standard double bourbon, I a bottle of Beck's. We both ordered the special of the day, Wiener schnitzel, cottage fries, buttered carrots, and a tossed green salad.

Over our coffee, he said, "I'm bushed. I spent most of last

night driving to San Valdesto after the funeral. Maybe only one or two stops tonight?"

"Fair enough. It's been a tiring day for me, too. How about this Fernando Valdez, the guitarist? His address isn't far from here."

"Let's go."

The residence of Fernando Valdez was not a house; it was a converted garage. A long shelf loaded with flowers in pots ran the length of the overhead door. A battered Dodge pickup truck was on the driveway.

The entrance was on the side of the building. There was no bell. Harley knocked.

The tall, thin Chicano youth who opened the door was wearing blue cords and a blue work shirt. His long black hair was gathered in a ceramic ring at the back. He was barefoot.

Harley said, "I'm Jasper's father and this is a friend of mine. We're investigating Jasper's . . . death."

"Come in," the youth said.

His dining table was a steel card table, a campers' stove sat on a table nearby. His bed was an army cot. His clothes were on hangers, strung on a long pole at the far end of the room. There were three chairs for visitors. There was no bathroom or any faucet in sight.

Harley said, "We're trying to learn the true name of a man who calls himself Big Bear. We haven't had much luck."

"Neither did any of us," Fernando said. "I'm sure he had more than one name. I suspect he had a police record and that could be why."

Harley said, "He seemed to be admired in your group."

"Not by me. He was the one who put Jasper on the hard stuff. Your son, Mr. Belton, never touched the stuff until that creepy bastard put him on it. That's more than I can say for the rest of Duane's friends."

"Duane told us Big Bear left town owing him seventy dollars."

64

Fernando smiled. "That's peanuts to Duane. His mama sends him a big fat check every week. She lives in Beverly Hills and he lives in *Venice!* Gringos!" He smiled again. "Nothing personal, gentlemen."

"No offense taken," Harley said. He took a five-dollar bill from his wallet and handed it to Fernando. "There's nothing else you could tell us about Big Bear?"

Fernando shook his head. Then, "Wait. There was a woman he brought to one of Duane's parties one night. Damn it, I forget her first name! Her last name was Meredith and I remember the street she told me she lived on. It's Cervato Way but I can't remember if she told me the house number. She must have been about sixty and ugly as sin. There can't be too many people named Meredith on Cervato Way. It's only about three blocks long and ends at the beach."

"Thank you," Harley said.

"You're welcome. I hope you find that bigoted bastard. If you do, give him a shot for me."

"I will," Harley said. "Thanks, again."

Outside, he said, "I've had more than enough for today. Let's hit the sack."

I agreed.

CHAPTER 9

THE MORNING WEATHER REPORT ON THE RA-
dio could have been a taped replay of the standard San
Valdesto report: overcast in the morning, clearing by noon,
except along the coast.

At breakfast, Harley asked, "This Meredith woman first?"

I nodded. We had found the only Meredith listed on Cervato Way last night in the phonebook—*J. Meredith, 267 Cervato Way.*

I nodded.

"Your car or mine?" he asked.

"Mine. Traffic here is a little heavier than it is in Sun
City."

He sighed. "I get the message. When we go out together
my wife always insists on driving."

"Why don't you phone her before we take off?"

"Later," he said.

Two sixty-seven Cervato Way was an old one-story frame
house flanked by a small convenience store on one side and
an older two-story stucco house on the other.

A thin white-bearded man who could have been older
than either house was putting out his trashcan at the curb in
front of the larger house when we got out of the car.

"You guys cops?" he asked.

66

I shook my head. Harley said, "Why do you ask?"

"There was such a rumpus in there last night, I figured somebody must have complained. Such screaming—!"

"And you phoned the police?"

"Not me, mister! I got enough troubles of my own."

"Have you seen her this morning?" Harley asked.

The man shook his head. "But I see her morning paper is still on the sidewalk. She always picks that up early."

Harley looked at me and then at the house. I said, "Let's go up and find out."

We went up to the low front porch and rang the bell. No answer. A minute later, Harley rang it again. No answer. He tried the knob. The door was not locked.

"Should we go in?" he asked.

I nodded.

The narrow hallway ran the length of the house. The small living room was on the left as we entered, a smaller guest room on the right. Nobody was in either room. The bathroom on the left farther down the hall was also vacant. The kitchen and a small breakfast nook were at the rear of the house. Nothing.

There was another door at the left end of the kitchen. Harley opened it and we saw the steps going down. Basements are not common in Southern California. Harley flicked the light switch at the head of the stairs.

It wasn't a basement. It was a root cellar, an excavation about eight feet by eight feet with a dirt floor. Two large rats deserted the body they were feasting on and scurried into the area beneath the steps.

A woman was lying there, a thin woman in a yellow kimono. I couldn't guess her age by her face; her face was covered with blood.

"Jesus!" Harley said.

"We'd better phone the police," I said.

We were going down the hall toward the phone in the living room when the front door opened. A uniformed police

67

officer stood in the doorway, a wide and swarthy man with a gun in his hand.

"Stay right where you are," he said, "both of you! Turn around and put your hands on the wall and don't make any foolish moves. Put 'em up high."

A younger, thinner patrolman had followed him in. We did as requested as they frisked us.

"Okay," the swarthy officer said. "You can put your hands down now—but don't turn around!"

"We were heading for the phone when you came," I said. "My name is Brock Callahan. You can confirm that by my driver's license. You can also check me out with a phone call to Captain Aram Apoyan at your station. We were about to report to him that there is a dead woman in the root cellar. The doorway to it is in the kitchen."

"Phone the captain," he told the other officer. "I'll stay here."

I said, "If it was her neighbor who phoned you guys, he should have called last night when he heard her screaming."

"Did he tell you that?"

"He did. That's why we came in. The door wasn't locked."

"We'll get back to him," he said.

The younger man came back to tell his partner that Captain Apoyan had confirmed that he knew me and I was to report to him *immediately.*

The old man wasn't in front when we went out but four neighbors from across the street were standing on the walk, watching the house. Another police car pulled up as we drove away, plainclothesmen.

"That old coot could have saved her life," Harley said bitterly.

I didn't comment. It was a silent drive to the station.

Aram smiled at me as we entered his office. "The *odar* is back to haunt us. And this time it's breaking and entering."

Odar is the Armenian word for other, for the non-

68

Armenian. I said, "Entering, but not breaking. The door wasn't locked."

"A minor difference. And what is your interest in this woman who was killed, this Jane Meredith?"

"We think she might have been living with the man who killed Jasper Belton in San Valdesto. This is Jasper's father."

Aram's broad face became more somber. "I read about what happened, Mr. Belton, but the San Valdesto police never notified us he was here. If he is, I assure you the full cooperation of this department." He looked at me. "Is this the same man who threatened you?"

I nodded.

"Why?"

"I don't know. I don't even know who he is. I suspect it might be some man I put away when I was working down here."

He took a deep breath. "Wait here. I'll see if any reports have come in to Homicide."

He came back five minutes later. Nothing, he told us. None of the neighbors knew the man's name. He had been living, off and on, with Jane Meredith for the last month. Evidently, she wasn't a socializer.

"And," he added, "the detective who frisked you both reported that neither of you was carrying a gun. Weren't you taking a big risk?"

"I guess," I admitted. "I didn't bring mine and I don't think Harley has one. I rarely carry a gun, as you must remember."

"Well, that's one plus for your side. What else have you learned while you were in town?"

Harley put our list on Aram's desk. "Here are some of the people who knew my son and also this man we're looking for. You may copy it, if you wish."

"I wish," Aram said. "I'll be right back."

He came back about ten minutes later. "We'll check out

these names and I'll also phone San Valdesto. Where are you two staying?"

"At the Bayside Inn. If we're not there, leave a message."

He promised us he would and warned us to be careful.

It was a tedious and unproductive trip from then on. We were told what we already knew or told nothing by the resentful kids who probably considered us establishment citizens. Three of them weren't home; they worked days.

We stopped in to see Aram on the way back to the motel. I told him what I should have told him earlier, about the Corinth cigarettes. So far as I knew, I explained, they were a rare brand. If they were available in town, a stakeout of the stores that sold them might be a wise move.

He agreed.

In the car, Harley said, "Back to San Valdesto? I can't believe that jerk would stay here when he's as hot as he is now."

"We'll stay over," I said. "We still have three places to go tonight."

In the room, he said, "I'm going out for a run on the beach. The only thing we've been exercising is our mouths."

"Did you bring running shoes?"

"Everywhere I go."

I was trying to find a pattern in all that I had learned since my trip to Tritown when Aram phoned around four o'clock. They had located a store that had sold Corinth cigarettes to a man that fit Big Bear's description. "But we got there an hour late," he said.

"He'll probably be back."

"Maybe not. He bought two cartons. And something else. We learned that Jane Meredith withdrew five hundred dollars from her savings account yesterday but we didn't find a plugged nickel in the house. The man now has traveling money."

"If he got it from her, why would he kill her?"

"Our best guess is that she learned his real name, somehow. Are you staying in town?"

"At least for tonight. We still have to talk to three people who weren't home today."

"We can handle that. What are their names?"

"Aram, you know what we both think of your night watch!"

"Shit, yes! Okay. But report to me tomorrow."

"Of course."

Harley came in five minutes later, soaked in sweat. I relayed the information Aram had given me. "They were twenty minutes from catching him in San Valdesto," I pointed out, "and missed him by an hour here."

"The bastard can't stay lucky forever," he said. "I think I'll call my wife after I take a shower."

"Do that. I'm going down and have a poolside drink and study the girls in their bikinis."

There were no girls in the pool. That wasn't the reason I sat there with a bottle of Beck's. Harley Davidson Belton, I was sure, would not be as sentimental as he should be if I had stayed to overhear his conversation.

All that I had learned since Tritown should be enough to convince Tom Mallory and Chief Harris that they had a very doubtful case on Corey. But nothing I had learned was going to divert Big Bear from his mission. Maybe, as Harley had said, he couldn't stay lucky forever. Neither could I. I had learned with the Rams that the best defense is a strong offense.

Harley brought a Manhattan from the bar with him when he came out to join me. "Where are the girls?" he asked.

"I scared them all away."

He took a sip of his drink and stared out at the pool. "There were plenty on the beach. And too many in my Marine years. That's not the kind of training that builds a faithful husband, is it?"

"Nope."

"Maybe the kids are right. Try before you buy is the way they go these days."

71

"We did, too. At least I did. But we never called our pre-nuptial pussy a meaningful relationship."

"An adulterous husband and a bad father, that's what I've been. I'm going to make it up to her, Brock."

"Did you tell her that on the phone?"

"I did."

"I'm glad you did," I said. "Welcome to the club."

He smiled. "You must have *some* wife!"

"More than I can handle," I admitted.

I phoned her before dinner and told her I wouldn't be home tonight. She told me that Corey was still being held but Nowicki was sure he would soon be released on minimum bail. Otherwise, all was quiet on the San Valdesto front.

Nowicki must have learned from Harris or McClune what Aram had told them about Big Bear's most recent kill. Neither Harris nor Mallory was likely to want his public image tarnished by jailing an innocent young man who had been framed. They could reasonably assume that what I had learned could be disputed successfully in court. But never the word of a fellow officer with Aram's reputation.

We started with the farthest address after dinner, a duplex outside of Santa Monica on National Boulevard, near the old Douglas aircraft plant.

This was the address of the poet on the list, a name I've forgotten now. When he invited us into his living room, there were four other youths there who retreated to the kitchen. They could have been fellow poets; they were all thin and looked hungry.

The remaining bard had little to tell us. He, like Fernando, did not have a high opinion of Big Bear, nor of Duane. The only reason, he explained, that he had gone to Duane's parties had been economic; he stuffed himself there and his host had let him take leftovers home. It was his devout belief that Duane's mother's money could be put to better use by supporting the arts.

In the car, Harley asked, "Do you read much poetry?"

"Not often."

"My wife does," he said. "I'd better bone up on it."

"Don't go too far, Harley. One step at a time."

Nobody answered the bell at our second address.

The third was a small building in Venice. An outside stairway led to the second-floor entrance. We could hear an argument going on inside before Harley knocked on the door.

When the door opened, a short but very wide and ugly man in a tan jacket and maroon slacks glared at us. "What the hell do you want?" he asked.

"A lad named Deke Bishop," Harley answered. "Is he in?"

"Get lost!"

"I'm here," a voice from behind him said.

The man turned and said, "Shut up, punk!"

The turn had been his error; Harley put a hand on his back and sent him stumbling into the room. When he turned around again, Harley grabbed him by the throat with his left hand and was about to land a right-hand haymaker.

"Don't!" I said.

He shoved the man against the wall. "You stay right there, Shorty," he said, "or I'll throw you down those steps outside."

I asked young Bishop, "What's all the fuss about?"

"I owe him some money."

"For what"

"I don't want to say."

"Drugs?"

He looked at Shorty and back at me. "Are you guys cops?"

"We're working with them," I said. "But we don't always work the same way they do, as you must have noticed. My impetuous partner is Jasper Belton's father and that is why we are here."

He said nothing. He looked at Shorty and Harley and back at me.

"How much do you owe him?" I asked.

"Thirty dollars."

I took a ten and a twenty from my wallet and showed them to Shorty. "Come with me," I said, "and this will be yours. My friend and I prefer to talk in private."

He nodded.

I walked down the steps with him to his car at the curb in front of mine. His was a green Pontiac Grand Prix. I told him, "Stay away from that kid. You came awful close to winding up in intensive care tonight. I can't always control my partner."

He nodded again.

I jotted down his license number on the back of our list. "I have your number now. My name is Brock Callahan. You can check me out with Captain Aram Apoyan at the Santa Monica station." I gave him the thirty dollars. "Now go!"

He left. I went back up the steps. Deke Bishop was sitting on his bed at the far end of the room.

Harley said, "Nothing new here. And Deke doesn't want to tell me that man's name. He's a pusher."

"I have his license number. What is he selling you, Deke?"

"Nothing. I quit a month ago. But I still owed him."

"Not any more. I'm sure he won't be back."

"If you'd give me your address," Deke said, "I could pay you off at ten bucks a week. I'm working now."

"No need, son. You stay clean and I'll be more than repaid."

"I promise," he said.

Back in the car, Harley said, "Thanks for stopping me. That's all I need, to wind up in the can for assault."

"You're welcome. I was almost as wild when I worked down here."

"And then you moved to San Valdesto and I to Sun City. That should have cured us."

"Not in San Valdesto, as you have reason to know."

"Jesus, yes! What's happening to this country, Brock?"

"A national epidemic of self-interest."

"Whatever. We're nowhere, aren't we? Only one name left and I'll give you ten to one it's another dead end."

"Probably. I may as well go home and wait for him to call."

"Your case is different. He's out to get *you*. But I'm out to get *him*. I don't want to wait."

We were getting out of the car on the parking lot when a green Pontiac Grand Prix pulled in.

"If that's Shorty's car," I said, "I hope he's not armed."

CHAPTER 10

IT WAS SHORTY. HIS HANDS WERE VISIBLE AND neither one held a gun. "Could I talk with you guys?" he asked.

I nodded. "What's your name?"

"If you got my license number you can get my name. Do you want to see my driver's license?"

"We do."

He took out his wallet and handed it to me. His name was Leonard Pelch.

"How did you know we were staying here?" I asked.

"I followed you. How else? Look, I've already had three raps and I'm out on probation now. You give my name to Apoyan and I'm right back where I don't want to be. I knew you son, Mr. Belton. But I never sold him anything. I'm a dealer, not a pusher. All I do is supply the demand."

"We'll buy that for now," Harley said. "What do you want from us?"

"I thought maybe I could help you. I've been working this town for twenty years. I've seen that creep the kids call Big Bear, the guy your son left town with. I don't know his real name, but I have friends who might. They figure this is *their* turf. That's probably why he took off for San Valdesto."

I shook my head. "He came up there to kill me. I think he

killed Jasper because Jasper was going to inform on him. Apoyan thinks that's the same reason he killed that woman he was living with, Jane Meredith."

Pelch stared at me. "Christ! Maybe I'd be better off if you finked to Apoyan. I didn't know the guy was *that* heavy!"

"If you can help, Lenny, neither Apoyan nor Big Bear will learn anything from us."

"What if I try and can't deliver?"

"Then we'll give you an E for effort. You know our names."

"Are you the Callahan who played for the Rams?"

"One and the same."

"Your word's good enough for me," he said. "That goes for you, too, Mr. Belton."

"That's a sweet thought, Lenny," I said. "But if we find out that youre conning us—"

"I should live so long!"

"It wouldn't be long," Harley assured him.

Lenny left. Harley said, "I think I understand now what you meant about self-interest. But we have to have some of that in us, don't we?"

"If we want to survive," I admitted. "Should we have a nightcap?"

"Why not? We earned it today. Maybe even two?"

We had one. The bar was full of loud men and middle-aged women. "I wasn't planning any moves," Harley said, "but I thought we could at least look at some of the young ones. Let's go up and see what's on the tube."

There was, as usual, nothing worth watching on the tube. We went to bed, each in his own.

Jan phoned before breakfast. She gave me the good news that Corey was out on bail and living at our house. She had paid the five hundred dollars for a five-thousand-dollar bond and Corey was working it off. We were also saving two-thirds of what the guards had been costing us; she had retained only one watch, from eleven at night to seven in the morning. And she was back at work.

"Don't you think that's risky?"

"No. Bernie drives me down every morning on his way to the station and brings me home every afternoon."

"Considering how much you like Bernie," I said, "I'm not sure I approve."

"We have kept our relationship on a high intellectual plane, sir," she said. And added, "So far. Anything new down there?"

I told her I had planned to come home this morning but we had received some information last night that might help us here.

"Luck," she said. "Don't you worry about Bernie. And I won't worry about all those girls you used to court down there."

"Until I met you. Remember that!"

"That's what I'm remembering."

Harley suggested at breakfast that I stay in the hotel in case Pelch called. He would try to learn something from the neighbors about the resident of the third house—the unanswered ring.

I wanted to suggest that we switch roles. But it had been his idea. "Drive carefully," I cautioned him.

I bought a copy of the *Times* and went up to the room. I couldn't concentrate on the print. All the people I had met, all those names, kept running through my mind. A tidbit here, another there, learning almost everything about Big Bear but his true name. He had to be on the run, either an escapee from prison or a man who had violated his parole. He hadn't revealed his true name to anyone we had questioned; if there was a price on his head, a reward for his capture, Lenny's criminal associates were not likely to have learned it.

I phoned Aram and asked him if he had gone through his mug shots. All of them, he told me, and they had reviewed all the wanted posters they had. They were still keeping a watch on the tobacco store in town that sold Corinth cigarettes.

The man had to be sadistic. Why the warning? Why this cat and mouse? Without the warning I would have been an easy target and his mission would now be accomplished. But the dead don't suffer; that is reserved for the living. He wanted me to sweat.

I went back to the *Times*. The front page informed me that the Valley Intruder had pleaded innocent to all charges. The sports page revealed that the Dodgers were on a losing streak, the Angels breaking even, a win for each loss. The financial page gave me the sad news that, like the Dodgers, I was also on a losing streak.

At ten o'clock I told the clerk that I would be out at the pool if any call came in. I took a bottle of Beck's with me.

They were mostly kids in the pool, laughing and splashing in the shallow end, innocents. And tomorrow, even if they stayed innocent, the ghost of that mushroom cloud would be hovering overhead. That could be the major reason that their high school siblings were so heavily into drugs.

I was in the room when Harley came back. It had taken him almost two hours to locate our last juvenile hope and only minutes to learn we now knew no more than we had known.

"We still have Lenny," I pointed out.

"Do you trust him?"

"I trust his sense of self-interest. Patience, man!"

He stretched out on the bed. "It was so simple in the Corps. Your superior told you what to do and you did it—or wished you had. They run an orderly world. But this—this dog eat dog—" He took a deep breath.

I thought of pointing out that prisons also ran an orderly world. But I said, "It's called free enterprise. You've been out in it for five years, Harley."

"I know. I must be a slow learner."

"Let's eat lunch."

"I'd rather drink it," he said. "But that's another problem I had better watch. It was the only diversion we had in Sun City."

Lenny phoned when we were back in the room. There was a man named Vince Columbini, he told me, who ran a combination restaurant, bar, and bookie joint in town who might have some information on Big Bear. The place was named The Hangout. He gave me the address.

"But he won't be there until eight o'clock tonight. He had to go to Ventura on business. He remembers you. He's a Rams fan. It could be nothing—but I'm still asking around."

"That's good of you. Thanks, Lenny."

When I relayed the information to Harley, he suggested, "Why don't we take a run on the beach and then come back for a swim?"

"I didn't bring my running shoes or swimming trunks."

"There's a sports store a little more than a block from here. And for the swimming you could use my jock strap and your underwear shorts."

"They'll probably have swimming trunks there."

He nodded. "And my jock strap would probably be too big for you."

"What a funny, vulgar person you are!" I said.

They had swimming trunks and running shoes. I also bought a sweat shirt and wore it with a pair of well-worn cords I had brought for possible undercover work.

The afternoon had turned cool; the beach was thinly populated. Mr. Macho Marine set a fast pace for the outgoing two miles. I trailed behind, giving him a false sense of security.

On the return run, I edged closer, waiting for him to falter. His stride grew ragged in the last half mile. I turned on my supercharger and beat him by almost ten yards.

"You sure fooled me," he admitted. "A man your size!"

I smiled modestly.

"Let's go back and take a shower and splash around in the pool," he suggested. "We could use a change. I'm getting tired of running into dead ends."

We splashed around in the deep end while the young kids splashed around in the shallow. Then we stretched out on pads in the returning sun.

Why, I wondered, hadn't Big Bear made his move? I'd been out in the open enough. It had to be what I thought it was; he wanted me to sweat. I voiced this thought to Harley.

"If you mean at the beach," he said, "you were a moving target there. I learned that in the Marines: don't shoot at a moving target. Because if you miss, the next shot is theirs. And that creep doesn't have a license to kill. He isn't about to do it in front of witnesses. What he wants is you all by yourself. Let's not talk about him. We forgot that freak for a spell. This afternoon was fun, wasn't it?"

"We needed the break," I agreed.

Half an hour later he went up to phone his wife. I pulled my pad into the shade and tried to take a nap. It was hopeless; too many faces, too many questions, not enough answers.

I was about to go up to the room when a tall lean old man in jeans and a corduroy jacket came over to me. "The desk clerk told me you were out here," he said. "Are you Mr. Callahan?"

I nodded.

"My name is Amos Meredith. I'm Jane's brother. Captain Apoyan told me you were the one who found Jane. I thought maybe you might know something about the man she was living with."

"I know some things about him—but not his name. Did your sister know it?"

He sat down in a chair nearby. "No. And that could be the reason why—what happened happened. He told her his name was Bart Tuttle. Well, I only met him once when I was down here and I didn't like him. He told me then that he had worked at Reilly Cartage in Oxnard for two years. That's where Jane and I lived until she moved down here. And I learned from some of the old-timers at Reilly Cartage that *no* Bart Tuttle had *ever* worked there. I phoned Jane night before last and told her that. That could be why—"

His voice broke. He sniffled. He reached into his jacket pocket, took out a handkerchief and blew his nose.

I said quietly, "Your sister wouldn't be the first, Mr. Meredith."

I went on to tell him about Jasper Belton and the notes I had received. "Jasper's father and I are looking for the man right now."

"I hope you find him," he said. "I hope he gets what he deserves." He shook his head. "But when I think about some of the creatures the courts have turned loose lately—"

"Not this time," I said—and almost believed it.

He left. I sat and remembered that scene Harley and I had come upon, that thin old woman with the bloody face being nibbled by rats. Amos was right; the courts had turned loose some strange creatures. Not this time, I tried to tell myself. . . .

Harley was watching the tube when I went up to the room. The picture showed a nine-story hotel that had collapsed, all the top floors now resting on the floor below them.

"A seven point eight earthquake has hit Mexico City," he told me. "They don't know how many thousands have died. Jesus!"

The horror story went on, scene after scene. Mangled infants were now being carried from the rubble.

"Enough!" I said and turned off the set.

I told him about my visit from Amos Meredith and what he had told me.

"Do you think Bart Tuttle is his real name?"

"I don't. The kids are one thing, but the woman he lived with sure as hell wouldn't settle for Big Bear."

"Right." He sighed. "Thank God we had our afternoon in the sun. The picture of that woman lying there in the dirt— and those rats! And then those pictures on the tube! It could put a man over the edge. I'm going to have a stiff drink with my dinner. We didn't have any at lunch."

"I'll have one, too. Should we try that place that Lenny mentioned, The Hangout?"

"As long as they have booze, why not?"

It looked like my kind of place, red-and-white-checked ta-blecloths on rough wooden tables, a bottle of ketchup hold-ing center stage on each of the tables. There were two male waiters in shiny black suits and black bow ties, one waitress in a short black skirt and a well-filled white blouse.

We both ordered double bourbon over ice. There was more bourbon than ice, a welcome change from our motel bar. Harley ordered spaghetti and meat balls. I ordered fet-tucini with clam sauce.

When the waiter brought our coffee, I asked, "Is Mr. Co-lumbini here yet? My name is Brock Callahan."

"He'll be here by the time you finish your coffee, Mr. Cal-lahan. He's expecting you."

He came to our table when we finished our coffee. "Mr. Columbini will see you now."

We followed him down a narrow hallway past both rest rooms to a small office at the end. The door was open. We went in. He closed the door.

The walls were paneled in cedar, the wall behind the desk crowded with photographs, some of them signed. Deacon Jones, Crazy Legs Hirsch, Bob Waterfield, Tom Fears, Tank Younger, Norm Van Brocklin, and on to the newer Ram stars and our current superstar, Eric Dickerson.

Columbini stood up from behind his desk, a man as short and wide as Lenny but not quite as ugly. His stiff hair was iron gray. "The Rock!" he said. "Finally!"

He picked up a photograph from his desk and a pen. "Please?"

"Of course," I said.

When I had autographed it, he hung it on one of the few bare hooks on the wall and said, "Sit down, gentlemen."

We sat in a pair of straight-backed chairs near his desk. He said, "I've been phoning around since Lenny told me what you wanted. I'm sorry to say that I haven't come up with much."

"Neither have we. This is Jasper Belton's father."

"I guessed that. I mean to help as much as I can, Mr. Belton."

Harley nodded. "Thank you."

"From my reliable sources," Columbini told us, "I learned that this man is a compulsive gambler and a steady loser. His favorite gambling game seems to be craps. We don't have much of that in town. I also learned that he once mentioned a younger brother who was in prison, but that was some time ago. From my less reliable sources, but still a logical guess, he also must have been in prison and escaped or possibly violated his parole."

"That's my guess, too," I said. "Especially if there's a reward out for his capture."

"Exactly. Unfortunately, that's all I have learned. I've exhausted my sources of information."

I thanked him and we left. In the car, Harley said, "He talks like a banker and he's a bookie."

"They're both in the money game," I explained. "We've probably learned all we can here. He could be up in San Valdesto now."

"Not while you're here and your house there is guarded."

When we came into the motel, the desk clerk told me somebody had left a message. It was an envelope without a stamp or postmark, only my name typed in capital letters.

The file card inside was also typed: *You're getting closer. Start digging your grave.*

CHAPTER 11

SEVEN WORDS AGAIN. I ASKED THE CLERK, "Did you see the person who left this?"

He shook his head. "I was in the washroom. It was on the counter when I came back. But one of our guests told me he saw the boy who put it there. He didn't get a glimpse of his face, only his back. He was a skinny black kid. Trouble, Mr. Callahan?"

I nodded. "A threat."

Harley said, "It was probably some kid he saw outside and paid to bring it in."

The clerk asked, "Should I phone the police?"

I shook my head. "Not if we can't identify the boy. We're working with the police."

"And you have no idea of who might have sent it to you?"

"Everything but his name," I said. "If we get any phone calls be sure not to give the caller our room number."

He assured me that it was house policy to give no caller or visitor a guest's room number.

In the room, Harley asked, "How in hell did he learn that you're still here?"

I shrugged. "But we know he's here now."

"We should. But with a kook like him, how can we be sure?"

This was Friday. I said, "We'll stay over tomorrow and hope we have better luck. Then I'm going home. Let him come to me."

"I'll be going there, too," he said. "I'll be at the Sheraton."

"Nope. You'll stay at our house. I need you around, buddy."

"I'll bet your wife will love that."

"She won't complain. I guarantee it."

He went over to the windows and looked down. "There's no way he can climb up here. I think we should move one of our beds in front of the door."

We did that. Then he went to his grip and took out a big black Colt .45-caliber semiautomatic. "One of us has to be armed," he said.

"Both of us are," I told him. "I lied to Apoyan."

Fatigue and frustration fought each other in me when I went to bed. Fatigue finally won; I fell asleep.

Harley was shaving in the morning when I woke up. He had pulled his bed away from the door and the complimentary copy of the morning *Times* was lying on it.

Chief Chandler Harris had weaseled himself some big-city ink. He had explained in an interview with a *Times* reporter that the Meredith murder in Santa Monica and Jasper's murder in San Valdesto had undoubtedly been committed by the same man. He went on to compare it with the Valley Intruder.

Sheriff McClune, when interviewed by the same reporter, said simply, "I think we should wait until all the facts are in."

When Harley came out I asked, "Did you read this?"

He nodded. "When I was there, McClune told me Harris was more politician than cop."

"He told you the truth. Harris ran for Congress two years ago and got swamped. Maybe he's running for governor now."

86

"I liked McClune," he said.

"He's a good cop," I agreed, "and content to be just that."

"And I was content to be a good Marine," he said. "But that's not easy to explain to a wife, is it?"

"I guess not. I had to get solvent before I got married."

Apoyan didn't work on Saturdays. His weekend substitute did and we were semi-friends. Harley stayed at the motel to take any calls. I took last night's warning to the station.

"There probably won't be any useful fingerprints on it," I explained, "but it should mean the man is still in town, shouldn't it?"

He shook his head. "We had a call at four o'clock this morning from Ventura. Jane Meredith's Pontiac was found abandoned there. The plates had been changed but the registration slip was still in the glove box. That's pretty dumb for a car thief."

I told him what we had learned last night without mentioning Columbini's name.

"I suppose, as usual, you aren't going to give me the name of your source?"

"I would if I could. But I don't know it. I got the information over the phone."

He smiled. "You know, Brock, if anybody else had told me that he'd wind up in the sweat box. But I know what a stubborn bastard you are. How are you and Chief Harris getting along?"

"Not as well as I got along with you and Aram."

"I can imagine. What's he running for now—senator?"

"He doesn't confide in me. Give my best to Aram. I'm going home."

"If you intend to make a stop in Ventura, I'll put in a call for you."

"Thanks. But I'm sure he's heading for San Valdesto."

Harley was reading the paper when I came to the room. I

told him what I had learned and that I thought it was time to head for home.

He agreed.

"You can follow me," I told him. "Most good drivers agree that the proper distance for the following car should be one car length for each ten miles per hour of speed."

"Yes, sir!" he said and saluted.

There was no way he could follow that procedure. The Ventura Freeway was jammed and the sports-car pukes kept switching lanes, crowding into any open space that gave them a clearance of more than six inches, slowing the normal flow of traffic as the citizens backed off to give them room.

His Camaro went zipping past soon after we left Oxnard. Sixty miles later he was waiting for me at the Montevista turnoff.

From there up the long winding road to home he maintained the good-driver distance.

Corey was sitting in a deck chair in the shade at the north side of the house, keeping his eagle eye on the road in front. He came over as we drove in.

I introduced him to Harley and asked, "Is Jan home?"

He shook his head. "I took her to work this morning before the guard left. Vogel doesn't work on Saturdays."

"I thought the guard left at seven o'clock?"

"Not today. Mallory has decided I'm not a suspect. I cost you money, Brock; you don't have to pay more for security. I'll watch the place."

I was tempted to remind him that he was the one who was paying for the bond by working for me. But that would have spoiled a happy homecoming.

Mrs. Casey was preparing lunch in the kitchen. "Thank God you're home!" she said.

"I brought a guest for lunch. He'll probably be staying over."

"That's all right. Just so *you're* home."

Harley went out to try the pool after lunch. Corey went

88

back to his vantage point, taking a paperback mystery along. I stayed in the house, recording all I had learned on the trip. The pattern of the man was beginning to emerge.

Leaving Jane Meredith's registration slip in her car could be another of his ploys, luring me to a fruitless hunt, stretching out my sentence of apprehension and frustration.

He knew where we were staying in Santa Monica but had not made his move. Why not? If I was his target, why not? I knew why, damn him! I put the papers away and went out to the pool.

Harley was sitting on a pad in the sun. He told me, "I've decided I'll stay here only for tonight, Brock."

"You're going home?"

"No. I'll stay at a hotel."

"This is a lot cheaper than the Sheraton."

"I don't plan to stay there. Big Bear isn't likely to show there. I'll find some place in his kind of neighborhood. As I explained to you before, he's out to get you and I'm out to get him."

"That's rough country down on lower Main Street."

"Brock, please! That's the kind of country we headed for every time we got a weekend pass. You have Corey here. You don't need me."

"Okay. Your best bet would be the Travis Hotel if you're allergic to roaches and bedbugs. That was the last place of residence of Big Bear when he was in town."

The local afternoon paper informed us that there had been another earthquake in Mexico City, a 7.3 jolt this time. It also informed us that the Los Angeles police were on the hunt for another weirdo, labeled the Serial Killer, a man who specialized in knifing prostitutes. Two of the ten women he had attacked had survived. When (and if) they recovered enough to talk, the L.A. police hoped to get a description. Chief Chandler Harris's two-victim slayer could now be relegated to the want-ad pages.

Jan gave me a big kiss and a tight hug when she came home. I introduced her to Harley.

She said, "You boys must be bushed. I'll make the drinks. I'll take a bottle of Einlicher out to Corey first."

"I'll have the same," I said.

"What's Einlicher?" Harley asked.

"America's finest beer. That's what I was drinking at Heinie's."

"Make it three," he said and smiled at Jan. "Please."

When she left, Harley said, "No wonder you don't mess around! You hit the jackpot, buddy."

I changed the subject. "Maybe you ought to call your wife and tell her where you are."

"I will after dinner. She's in the rec hall now, playing bridge." He sighed. "Six days a week, afternoon bridge."

Corey was slated to eat in the living room, where he could watch the road. Harley suggested that he replace him this evening. Mrs. Casey seconded the suggestion. Jan didn't look happy about that. She likes to look at skinny men who are closer to her age.

Back to the routine: Mrs. Casey to her old movies, Jan to her samples, me to my records. Harley phoned his wife and then sat with Corey in the living room, yakking and watching.

It was another misty night. The lawn lights were on; the guard's car sat masked in the shadow of the garage and the shrubbery bordering the driveway.

Big Bear had a brother who had spent time in jail. *He* could be the man I might have put away. But my records weren't that complete; there had been no mention in them of a bald and scarred brother, or any reason to record it. At the time.

Mrs. Casey, since Corey moved in, had made an exception to her dictum of not making breakfast. She got up at six so he could have his breakfast before the guard left and she generously stayed up to serve us lesser mortals.

Harley left after breakfast. I drove Mrs. Casey to her ten-o'clock Mass. When I returned to the house a couple of teen-age boys were playing catch on the Crider lawn and there was a car with a Missouri license plate on their driveway.

"Do the Criders have visitors?" I asked Corey.

He shook his head. "They sold out and moved to Sun City."

They had found their sanctuary.

Jan was on the phone when I came into the house. When she hung up she told me she had invited the Vogels for dinner. "And your friend Bernie asked if he should bring his gun. I don't think that was funny."

"Bernie," I explained, "has to deal with hoodlums day in and day out. Most cops do. They have a less panicky view of the breed than we ordinary citizens do."

I told Corey after lunch that I would stand guard for a while and he could get some exercise in the pool. The sher-iff's cruiser went past three times in my first hour of watch. I joined Corey and Jan in the pool. Let the bald cat play his nitwit game; I was a man, not a mouse. Corey was no longer being held. Our family was alive and well. But Jasper Belton was neither well nor alive and Harley Davidson Belton was on the hunt. Baldy was overmatched—I tried to tell myself.

When the Vogels came, we all sat in the living room, no-body in the front yard. Over the expensive Scotch I reserve for Bernie's refined taste I related to him all that Harley and I had learned on the trip.

"So now," I explained, "we know everything about the killer except his name."

"Everything about the *suspect*," he corrected me, "except his name."

"Come on! He was living with Jane Meredith. She was beaten to death and five hundred dollars she had withdrawn from her savings is missing. Her car is found abandoned in Ventura. Corinth cigarette packages are found in the shack and in his hotel room, and I learned that's what he smokes.

91

We can tie the man up with Jasper. Are you telling me that's not a case?"

"It's reasonable cause for arrest," he admitted. "But where is the hard evidence? Any prowler could have killed Jane Meredith and stolen her car and her money. And you can be sure the defense attorney will have half a dozen people in court who smoke Corinth cigarettes. And where's the weapon? Corey's is the only one that has been found, and it matched the slug in Belton's neck. Think of what the defense can make of *that*."

"Corey's safe, isn't he?"

"He can be picked up again. Is this the last of your drinkable Scotch?"

"I'll bring you another," I said. "But you sure as hell haven't earned it."

"Brock," he said patiently, "I was only trying to point out what could happen. I'm sure you don't believe in vigilante justice."

"Of course not!" I half lied. "Neither Stan Nowicki nor I believe in that."

"Nowicki!" he said scornfully.

"You have just contradicted yourself," I told him.

"What in hell do you mean by that?"

"Mull it over," I said, "while I get you another free drink."

I don't know if he mulled it over or not while I was getting his drink. The fact in hard evidence is that he didn't reopen the discussion when I came back.

We changed pairings after dinner. Bernie and Jan talked about the new writers and artists I couldn't understand and Ellie didn't want to understand. Ellie and I talked about the various causes which were her present interest, all of them concerned with making this a better world, and I gave her a donation before they left.

The guard was on watch by that time. We all went to bed, except for Mrs. Casey, who was probably watching the late, late golden oldie movie on the tube.

CHAPTER 12

THE MORNING WAS OVERCAST BUT THE weatherman promised us a clearing by noon. Mrs. Casey made us popovers and a cheese omelette for breakfast.

Harley phoned after breakfast to tell me he was staying at the Travis Hotel. He had visited a couple of area bars the day before but had learned only that he should have worn shabbier clothes. I told him I had gone the route of them all before my trip to Los Angeles and learned nothing except that Big Bear had left town. I would come there in half an hour to have a strategy conference.

I took Jan to work on the way and parked in a lower Main Street municipal parking lot. I walked to the hotel from there.

The desk clerk told me that one of my two informants had managed to avoid the drunk tank this weekend and was in his room. I had never learned his last name; the other residents called him Sarge. The rumor on him was that booze had cost him both his family and a profitable accounting practice.

He was a man of about forty who could pass for sixty-five, thin and bony, with bloodshot blue eyes and sparse gray hair. When he opened his door he looked first at Harley and then at me. "What is it this time?"

"It's about a man wanted for murder. I noticed when I was here last week that his room was next to yours. The walls are thin and you have sharp ears."

"A big man? Bald and with a scar on his cheek?"

I nodded.

"He never had any visitors in his room that I heard. But I saw him outside one morning getting out of a blue Toyota pickup truck."

"Did you get the license number?"

He shook his head. "Why would I? I did notice that the frame around the license plate had a Ventura dealer's name on it. I don't remember the name."

"Do you remember what the driver looked like?"

He shook his head again. "He was in the cab and I only saw the back of the truck." He paused. "Is that worth a tenner?"

"Two fives," I told him. "The first five goes for a solid meal. You can spend the second one any damned way you please. Promise?"

His smile was cynical. "Man, you are really square, aren't you?"

"Guilty. Haven't I always been square with you?"

He nodded. "I promise."

I phoned the station from the pay phone in the lobby and told Bernie about the blue Toyota pickup. I suggested he pass it on to McClune.

He said he would, and added, "I suppose you don't want to give me your informant's name."

"Your supposition is correct," I said and hung up.

Harley said, "Jane Meredith's car was dumped in Ventura. Maybe we ought to go there."

"No. The way I see it, he dumped the car there because it was hot and maybe came up here in his friend's Toyota. He can't get to me by staying in Ventura. There's one more place I want to visit."

The place was Rubio's Rendezvous. Rubio hadn't been

there when I had made my previous canvass of the area. It was only two blocks from the hotel; we walked.

Rubio had a big smile for me. "Pancho!" he said. "Who's your friend?"

I introduced him to Harley and explained why we were here.

"I heard about your trouble," he said, "and Lieutenant Vogel gave me a description of the man. He was never in here." He smiled again. "I don't get many *gringo* customers."

"I've noticed that, except for me and The Judge. Has he been in lately?"

He sighed and shook his head. "We had a falling out. He isn't staying at the Travis Hotel any more. Somebody told me he is living with a niece in Omega."

Omega was a lower-middle-class suburb at the other end of town. I asked, "Politics, again?"

"*Sí.* He's so damned Republican! Pancho, I will ask around for you." He looked at Harley. "Take good care of our friend. He's—kind of hotheaded."

Harley winked and nodded.

Outside, he asked, "Where next?"

"I've run out of sources," I told him. "Now we can sit and wait. I'm going home."

"I think I'll cruise the town," he said, "and see if I can spot a blue Toyota pickup from Ventura."

"Okay. But drive carefully. We have a lot of one-way streets."

"I know," he said. "I almost got clobbered yesterday driving the wrong way on one."

Mrs. Casey was setting a card table on the driveway in front of the garage door so she could share lunch with Corey. She graciously agreed to set another plate for me.

The afternoon yawned at me after lunch. I decided to go out and visit with my old friend and mentor, Wallace Stanton. That was his name when he was not in Rubio's Rendezvous. There he was called The Judge, the arbiter of all in-house disputes except the political. I had to assume he would miss his former bar companions; he might enjoy a visit from one of them.

His name was not in the phone book. I called the Travis Hotel and got his forwarding address.

It was a small frame house at the end of a narrow road in Omega. The Judge was sitting in a wicker rocking chair under the shade of a pepper tree on his gray Bermuda-grass lawn. He didn't get up as I walked toward him. Three hundred pounds is a lot of weight to lift just to meet a guest.

"My friend!" he said. "What brings you here?"

"I come as a peacemaker."

"Blessed are the peacemakers," he quoted, "for they shall be known as the children of God." He frowned. "But I don't understand its application here. Surely you don't mean my spat with Rubio?"

"That's what I mean."

"That's nonsense! I moved out here to be with my niece. I don't have a car and neither does she." He pointed at the redwood bench next to his chair. "Sit down."

I sat. He said, "That Rubio is so petulant! You tell him I still consider him one of my dearest friends and explain my transportation problem."

"Why don't you?"

"We don't have a phone. So, how are things with you?"

"You shouldn't have asked," I said. I went on to give him the sordid history of my current travels and travail.

"A psycho," he said. "He'll probably find help down there. We've always had our criminal element. But the drifters from the big towns have been coming in. That's why I moved out. Our local Chicanos used to maintain a rough kind of vigilante order in the area. They had to, the skimpy police protection they were getting. But these newcomers—"

"The feeling I get about the man is that he wants to turn me into a nervous wreck before he makes his move."

"Who can read a warped mind? The reverse could be that he's trying to trigger you into making the fatal move. You're an impulsive man, Brock. Don't let your impatience make you the victim."

"I'm trying not to. McClune and Vogel have been cooperative and I'm having the house guarded. But without the man's name, the police department or the sheriff's men haven't enough to work with."

"Patience," he said. "Let us talk of other things."

We talked of other things; of our dangerous foreign trade deficit, our disastrous national debt, the recent spell of commercial airline crashes, the job his niece had at a local electronics firm, the Dodgers and the Lakers. We never got around to ships and shoes and sealing wax, nor cabbages and kings.

I didn't stay to meet his niece; I left before she came home.

I was heading for the freeway entrance when I saw a blue Toyota pickup turn into the frontal road. I followed it. When it was within viewing distance of the license plate frame I learned the dealer was a local agency.

Patience . . .

Corey was out in front, reading another mystery, the stalwart sentinel. I told him to go and get some exercise in the pool and took over his job.

I was still sitting there when Vogel brought Jan home. She went into the house; Bernie came over to where I sat.

"Anything new I should know?" he asked.

I shook my head.

"This is tough going for Jan," he said. "I don't think she should stay here."

I told him that had been my thought originally but neither she nor Mrs. Casey had agreed. "And, thinking about it now, she'd be even more vulnerable at some hotel than she is here. Want a drink?"

He shook his head. "Ellie is waiting to have one with me.

97

Don't play cowboy if you get a lead, Brock. This one is for cooler heads than yours or Belton's. Jan told me he's a retired Marine."

"And a tiger," I said. "I'll try to keep a leash on him."

"Be damned sure you do. This is police business."

"I know, I know! Don't keep Ellie waiting, Bernie."

I couldn't understand what he answered to that. He mumbled it to himself and walked to his car.

He had called it police business. It was a lawyer business. The police brought them in; the defense lawyers made their deals with the prosecutors so the court calendar wouldn't get more than two years behind. Our jails were overcrowded; the indignant (but penurious) citizens refused to have new jails built in their neighborhoods or vote for bonds to build them in any neighborhoods. So hard-core convicts had to be released to make room for the new ones.

And time off for good behavior—what in hell did that mean? It probably meant the criminal could walk out early if he promised not to attack the warden.

A major child molestation case was now in its twelfth month in Los Angeles. It involved a nursery school whose teachers were the defendants. Day after day the defense attorneys hammered at the young victims, confusing them, wearing them down, finally getting them to contradict themselves.

Dozens of the charges against the teachers had been thrown out of court. The defense attorneys' fees in that case alone could probably pay for a couple of new jails.

Maybe it was time for me to desert the ACLU.

Corey came out to tell me he would take over again. Jan was waiting for our pre-dinner drink.

She had our drinks ready. "You look owly," she said.

"I am."

"Another argument with Bernie?"

"A difference of opinion that I don't want to talk about."

"Then we won't. Bernie annoys me, too, at times. But he's your friend, Brock."

98

"Yes."

I went out to sit with Corey after dinner, taking a portable radio along so I could listen to the Dodgers game. In the middle of the fifth inning a gray Chevrolet two-door sedan stopped in front of the house. Corey went over to stand behind a shrub, his gun in hand.

The car's headlights went out, the front door opened, and I could see in the glow from the interior light that it was Rubio. "It's okay, Corey," I called.

He came out from behind the shrub as Rubio walked over. Rubio asked, "Is he a policeman?"

"No. He's a friend of mine, a private detective."

"Then he may listen to what I have to say. We had a meeting of the Brotherhood tonight, and a vote. The vote was unanimous. Our president sent me to tell you that we are going to find that man who is threatening you."

"You don't intend to cooperate with the police?"

"Never! They have jailed more of our people than they have protected. But you have been our good friend since you moved here. We owe you, *amigo*."

"I'm grateful," I said. "Hell, I'm *touched!* Thank you. Could you use a beer?"

"No, thank you. I have to get back to close the bar."

When he left, Corey asked, "What's the Brotherhood?"

"A Chicano group organized to keep their kids out of trouble and their adults out of jail. Their full name is the San Valdesto Brotherhood. I cleared their president of a murder charge on my last case. Chief Harris was determined to nail him."

The darling Dodgers beat the mean Giants, 4 to 2, on a grand-slam homer by Marshall with two out in the last half of the ninth inning. I went into the house.

"It's been a long time since we had cocoa," Jan said.

"I'm ready for it."

"Feel better now?"

"Some."

I decided not to tell her about Rubio's visit. We had our

99

cocoa with some of Mrs. Casey's chocolate chip cookies and went to bed.

It was a clear night for a change, with a full moon and a light breeze. Shadows from the maple trees in front of the window flickered through the room. But they were only shadows.

CHAPTER 13

LARRY RUBIN PHONED IN THE MORNING TO tell me he had another hot one at long odds running at Hollywood Park and did I want my usual double sawbuck riding on his nose?

I told him I did.

"What's this static I hear about you around town?" he asked. "Something about a weirdo."

"It's a long and complicated story," I said, "and I'm tired of repeating it."

"Vogel told me at the poker game that it might have something to do with that guy who was asking about you at Heinie's."

"It is. I went down there to check him out and got nowhere."

"Didn't I tell you to talk with me first? Didn't I tell you I have friends down there who could help you?"

"You told me," I admitted. "What's my horse's name?"

"Galloping Ghost."

"That's what they called Red Grange."

"Who's Red Grange?"

"Look it up. He might be the greatest running back who ever lived. He lived before your time."

"I am not a history buff," he said. "If you plan another trip to L.A. call me before you go."

"Okay!"

I didn't tell Jan about the bet. Larry doesn't *always* pick winners and if she split the bet with me and lost, she would sulk. She hates to lose at *anything*.

Vogel picked her up, Corey went out to his vantage point. I didn't go back to my records. I had them almost memorized.

My Chicano friends and both the city and county police were on the hunt. They had more sources and resources than I had. I had slept through the night but the fury and frustration in me had me down.

If my Chicano friends got to him before the police did he would have more scars to add to the one on his cheek. He could suffer the same fate as the cat that was thrown on our lawn.

I worked out with the weights and was dozing when Harley came. He had spent the afternoon before and part of this morning cruising the town with no success.

He asked, "Would you take me to that place where Jasper died?"

"Why? There is nothing there that will help us."

"I just want to see it," he said.

I took him there. It was as cluttered as it had been on my first visit. There were two new additions, a couple of empty wine bottles that had once contained a cheap local muscatel wine.

"Jesus!" he said. "This is what I brought him to."

"Don't think that way, Harley. Don't blame yourself. It can eat you up. It's happened. It's over."

"I know," he said wearily. "I've watched men die in worse places. But they died for a cause."

I said nothing.

"Maybe it's time for me to go home," he said. "We're not even sure he's in town."

"If he isn't, he will be." I told him about Rubio's message of last night. "We have some allies now who know the territory. And if you hadn't come to town with Jasper's letters we'd have known a lot less than we do."

Mrs. Casey insisted that he stay for lunch, it being her theory that no human being can stay healthy on restaurant food.

We were sitting with Corey in the front yard when the mailman came. Buried in the garbage mail was another envelope enclosing another file card. Both the envelope and the card were printed in pencil in capital letters: WELCOME HOME. NOW YOU CAN START SWEATING.

Seven words again. I handed it to Harley.

"I can't understand it," he said. "A town this size? He has to go out to mail the letter. He has to eat some place. He has to buy gas if he has a car. And *nobody* spots him!"

"He could have a friend who handles that. He's probably holed up."

Harley looked at the postmark. "At least we know he's in town. I'm staying over."

He left and I sat with Corey for another half hour and then went into the house. I was dozing when the phone rang an hour later.

It was Harley. "You'd better come down here. I think I'm in trouble."

"Down where—the hotel?"

"No. The police station."

"What happened?"

"Come down and find out. I need you, man."

I told Corey where I was going in the event Jan came home before I did. I took the inner route; the freeway was jammed, as usual. San Valdesto is probably the only city in California that has traffic lights on the freeway.

The desk sergeant told me that Harris and Harley and Vogel and an unidentified man were in Harris's office.

Portly, penguin-shaped Chief Harris was sitting at his desk, his ruddy face redder than usual. Vogel and Harley sat in straight-backed chairs next to the side wall. The unidentified man was sitting in a captain's chair near the desk. He was wearing a sweat-stained T-shirt, jeans, and a baseball cap. He was short and stocky and muscular. He had a bruise below his left eye and a badly puffed lower lip.

There was no other chair in the room. I asked, "What happened?"

Harris said, "Interfering in a murder case could be one of the charges."

Vogel said, "Chief—please!"

I asked Harley, "What happened?"

He told me he had been walking from the parking lot to the hotel when he saw a blue Toyota pickup with a Ventura dealer's license plate frame. The driver was just about to get into the cab.

"So I asked him if he had dropped off a friend at the Travis Hotel a week or so ago and he got lippy. I did, too. And then he took a swing at me." He shrugged. "I beat him to the punch—just as a squad car was passing."

I asked Chief Harris, "Have any of your officers interrogated this man?"

"Yes. For your information, Mr. Callahan, about a third of the Toyotas in town are bought in Ventura. There's a dealer there who sells for a lot less money than the local one."

"I can't believe that ratio applies to pickup trucks."

"Oh? You've made a survey?"

"Both Mr. Belton and I have for the last day and a half. This is the first one either of us has discovered."

"How interesting! And now will you explain why a pair of hotheaded amateurs should be involved in police business?"

"I resent being called an amateur, sir, considering the cases I have worked on with this department. I might point out that it was my information that kept you from making a serious mistake when you tried to railroad Corey Raleigh."

A shade of purple began to darken his red face. "Watch that damned tongue of yours, Callahan! That was Mallory's decision."

"The information I have is that you and Tom Mallory agreed that Corey was your number one suspect."

"At the time, yes. At that time, he was."

"Not to me. I apologize for using the word *railroad*. Has bail been set for Mr. Belton?"

"There has been no charge so there will be no bail. Get out of here, all three of you. Bernie, you stay here."

Bernie nodded. I told him, "I'll pick up Jan."

"She won't be going home for another hour."

"She will with me."

Outside, the unidentified man asked, "What in hell was that all about in there?"

"Murder," I said. "And my friend, here, is the father of the boy who was murdered."

"Hey! Shit, man, I'm sorry! I work for the dealer old lard-ass in there was yakking about. Could I buy you guys a beer?"

"I'm buying," Harley said. "I owe you."

"Nah, I've been having trouble at home and I'm not myself. My name is Gus Henshaw."

We introduced ourselves and shook hands with him and headed for the Alamo Café, half a block down the street. I explained that most of the customers there were Chicanos.

"They don't bother me," Gus said.

"I admire them," Harley said. "I served with many of them in the Marines."

Gus shook his head. "My first fight in over a month and I have to pick on a Marine!"

Over premium Mexican beer at the Alamo Café, Gus asked for more background on the series of events that had led to his swollen lip. We told him most of it.

"And that Pontiac," he asked, "that was deserted in Ventura, is that the car this guy you're looking for was driving?"

"Almost certainly," I said. "It belonged to a woman he was living with in Santa Monica. She was beaten to death."

He nodded. "I remember reading about that. Look, I know a couple of cops in Ventura and the boss has records of all our sales since he opened the agency. Maybe I could learn something, huh? I mean, if we compared our list of customers with the rap sheets the police have there could be a connection."

"That," I told him, "is very sound thinking. You have just earned yourself another beer."

I gave him my address and phone number before we left.

As Harley and I walked back to the police station parking lot I suggested he come to our house for dinner.

"Thanks, but not today. I'm still going to prowl around, maybe out in Omega. From what I've seen of it it shapes up as likely hideout country."

"Be careful. Don't get lippy again."

He smiled. "Why not? It's already given us an ally in Ventura."

When I came into Kay Décor, Jan said, "What a pleasant surprise! Where's Bernie?"

"He wanted to drop in on his girl friend before he went home. Are you ready to go?"

"I am. You're lying about Bernie, aren't you?"

"Of course! Let's go."

I didn't tell her why I was downtown and I was glad she didn't ask. She takes a dim view of fisticuffs.

She had her drink in the house. I took a couple bottles of Einlicher out of the fridge and went out to sit with Corey. I told him what had happened downtown, including Gus Henshaw's offer of help.

"We're building an army," he said, "and we still haven't learned the man's name. Maybe we never will."

"It took a lot of cops a lot longer than this to learn the name of the Valley Intruder."

"Sure. And he'll probably walk in two years. So will Big Bear, if we ever find him."

"Not if our Chicano friends find him first."

"Would you want that? It's bad law, Brock."

"I know! But maybe good justice?"

"I thought so at first but I've been thinking about it, sitting out here. And I've been wondering—could I use a gun to kill a man, no matter how much he deserved it? I'll bet Harley could."

"And has. Could you kill a man if he was about to kill you?"

"I don't know. I could shoot him, but maybe in the leg or some other place that's not fatal."

"Corey, that wouldn't be justice. That would be suicide. You can be damned sure that he's not going to aim for your leg."

He nodded in agreement. "And I've also been wondering if Big Bear carries a gun. He used mine to kill Jasper and to beat that woman to death in Santa Monica. If he has a record, he wouldn't be permitted to carry a gun, would he?"

"I'm not sure. We know he's not permitted to kill people."

Vigilante justice . . . Even my refined, liberally inclined Jan had been guilty of voicing it about the Valley Intruder. The old western movies I had grown up on were shoot-'em-outs, the current movies and boob-tube series had become even more violent. Allegedly literate and responsible citizens had voiced support of it. Conservative politicians had endorsed it, including our actor President.

Our Bill of Rights was under attack by the millionaire TV ministers, our schools hassled by rght-wing parents. A pregnant fourteen-year-old daughter was more acceptable to them than sex education in our schools.

All this I knew. But, still, there were times . . .

Patience, I told myself.

CHAPTER 14

LARRY RUBIN DROPPED IN BEFORE DINNER. My horse had won, but not at the morning odds we had hoped for. The payoff was sixty dollars and twenty cents. Deducting the twenty I owed Larry, that left me a net profit of forty dollars and twenty cents.

"And now," he said, "we will have a quiet cup of coffee and you will tell me about your troubles."

I shook my head. "Coffee only. We'll talk about something else."

"You bullheaded bastard! I have connections in Los Angeles you wouldn't even be seen with. I wouldn't be surprised if you had put away some of my best friends."

"Do they include killers?"

"I've known a few who might be, two of them Mafia. Get the coffee and we'll talk shop."

Jan was in the den, Mrs. Casey in her room. We drank our coffee in the living room. I gave him a truncated history of all the frustrated days I had spent since the dead cat was first thrown on our lawn.

"And he was asking for you at Heinie's? How would he know that used to be your hangout?"

I shrugged.

"It has to be some guy you put away, right?"

108

"Possibly."

"Did Heinie tell you what he looks like?"

"A very big man, bald, with a long scar down his right cheek."

"And you never tangled with a man like that? You put a lot of guys away, Brock."

"I know, I know! But I went through my records thoroughly and remembered what most of them looked like. But not this weirdo."

"I'm going to L.A. tonight," he said. "I'll look up some of my former—associates. They might know the man."

"Mafia associates?"

"Watch your tongue," he said. "Underworld, yes, that's where I spent my youth. So a couple of Mafia boys financed me when I started to book. That was before I knew what they were. I bought my way out of that connection."

"Okay, Larry. Walk carefully and carry a big schtick."

"A pun," he informed me, "is the lowest form of humor."

"That's where I am, low."

He left. I went back to my records. Nothing.

Jan came in to ask, "What did Larry want?"

"I owed him twenty dollars on a horse that didn't come through."

"I'm glad I didn't have half of it."

"So am I."

Dinner was quiet. Depressed might be a better word. Jan stayed up to watch the ten-o'clock news on the tube. I went to bed but couldn't sleep. Around one o'clock I took a couple of her sleeping pills. They helped. I was still sleeping when Vogel came to pick up Jan.

My pajamas were soaked with sweat. I took a hot shower, dressed, and went out to the kitchen.

Mrs. Casey was sitting in the breakfast nook. She doesn't make breakfasts, as I've mentioned, but she is a compassionate woman.

"Eggs?" she asked.

"Is there any of that Irish stew left over from last night?"

She nodded. "I'll heat it. Maybe, just this once, we ought to have a sip of Irish to quiet our nerves?"

"We ought to," I agreed.

She took her bottle from the cupboard. Good Irish whiskey and her famous Irish stew, and I was almost human again.

I was out at the pool, seeking nirvana, when the phone rang. Mrs. Casey had gone back to her room. I answered it.

It was Larry, calling from Los Angeles. He asked, "Do you remember that guy you put away named Glen Turbo?"

"Yes. He's in my records."

"Well, I played a little poker last night and I gave the boys your description of this guy you're looking for. One of them told me it sounded like Glen Turbo's brother. He was mostly a crap shooter. His name is Charles. The addicts call him Charley Seven."

"That could be the man," I said, remembering that all his threats were seven words long. "Thanks, Larry."

"You're *almost* welcome. I lost five big ones at the game!"

"You can afford it. Thanks, again."

Glen Turbo. I remembered that case. I had been hired by his wife to prove her charges of wife-beating and child molestation. I had testified in court for her.

I phoned Sheriff McClune and told him what I had learned.

"That could be a lead," he said. "Do you have a record on this Charles Turbo?"

"No. Only on his brother. He got five years at Fulton. He might have been paroled by now."

"The way things are going these days, he could have been paroled in six months. I'll phone Fulton and get back to you."

Vigilante justice and courtroom law fought a brief battle in me before I phoned Ricardo Cortez, head honcho of the Brotherhood. I told him what I had learned.

110

"Gracias, amigo," he said.

"Remember now, you take whatever you learn to the police."

"We always do," he lied.

It was Ricardo Cortez I had cleared of a murder charge on my last case. The Brotherhood was a necessary evil in their domain; they didn't get the police protection they needed under bigoted Chief of Police Chandler Harris.

We now had a name to go with the man's description and we had a motive. His guilt was not a certainty. But all I had learned made Charley (Seven) Turbo the odds-on choice for the man the kids knew only as Big Bear.

Sheriff McClune phoned back before lunch to give me the information he had picked up at Fulton. Glen Turbo was dead. He had been killed by his fellow prisoners.

"Even the hard-core cons can't stomach child molesters," he said. "Though he was raped a number of times before they knifed him."

"When was he killed?"

"Two months ago. If he had lived another week, he would have had a parole hearing. This Charles Turbo looks like our man, doesn't he?"

"He does to me."

"Don't go off half-cocked now, Brock. Don't do anything foolish."

"I'll try not to."

"I'll alert Vogel."

"Thank you."

Don't go off half-cocked. . . . Where had he learned what he now knew? He had learned it all from me. As for the city police, Corey would now be scheduled for trial if Chief Harris and District Attorney Mallory had prevailed. Don't go off half-cocked . . .

My record on the Glen Turbo case showed that he had had two children, Glen Junior, aged fourteen, and a daughter named Dianne, aged six. She was the girl he had molested. His wife, Eileen, was the woman he had battered. Dianne would now be nine, young Glen seventeen. They had lived in Santa Monica.

I phoned the Santa Monica station and Aram was there. I told him what I had learned since leaving his town.

"I remember the case," he told me. "His wife and kids moved out of town after the trial. I don't blame them, the shame they must have felt. I'm not sure, but I think they moved to Ventura. Should I call the chief there?"

"No. I'll do it."

"Okay. But remember that we want him here, too, on that Meredith murder. You keep me informed."

"Of course, Aram. Haven't I always?"

"No. But this time—"

"I'll keep you informed," I promised.

I didn't phone the Ventura police. I phoned the Toyota agency and asked for Gus Henshaw.

He was, the lady who answered informed me, out on a service call. But he should be back within the hour.

"Please have him phone me as soon as he gets back. I live in San Valdesto. My name is Callahan and he knows my phone number. Tell him to phone me collect."

"I will, sir. But if it's some trouble you're having with your Toyota, I could connect you with our service manager."

I assured her that I had never had trouble with any of my Toyotas; this was a personal matter. I didn't tell her I drove only Fords.

Gus phoned twenty minutes later. He said, "I haven't had time to check the records, Brock, but—"

"Look for the name Glen Turbo," I interrupted.

"I don't have to look for it. I know it. The pickup is registered in his mother's name but he's the one who drives it."

"Eileen Turbo?"

"That's right. They moved up here about three years ago from Santa Monica. The truck is blue. What's this all about?"

112

"He's the nephew of the man Harley and I are trying to find."

"Oh, boy! Should I alert one of my cop friends?"

"No. I don't want him heckled by the law. Give me his address."

"That would be better," he agreed. "He's a real nice kid. Just a second."

He gave me the address a few minutes later and the section of the town it was in.

I told Mrs. Casey I wouldn't be home for lunch and told Corey where I was going and why.

"Are you taking your gun?" he asked.

"Of course not! What's the danger?"

He shrugged. "I don't know. I feel nervous without it even when I'm in the shower."

"Don't tell me you're running scared."

He smiled. "I'm scared. But I'm not running, Brock. Good luck, boss."

Traffic was sparse on the freeway once I left the stop-and-go lights of San Valdesto behind. It probably would have been wiser to phone before going to Ventura; but a phone call might have spooked the lad. There was a possibility he wouldn't want to talk with the man who had put his father away.

The address Gus had given me was on the other side of the street from the direction I was traveling. It was a small stucco house in a neighborhood of small stucco houses. A thin youth in cutoff jeans and rubber thongs was washing a blue Toyota truck on the driveway.

He turned to face me as I walked the street. He frowned. "Mr. Callahan. Is that you?"

I nodded.

"I knew it. I think about you a lot," he said. "It was because of you that Mom and I have finally found some peace. Why are you here?"

"I'm trying to find your uncle."

113

"Uncle Charles?"

"That's the man. He doesn't share your opinion of me. I live in San Valdesto now."

He stared. "So that's why the bastard had me take him there! He's kooky, Mr. Callahan."

"He's worse than that. He's a suspect in two murders. The way it's shaping up, I'm next on his list. I was wondering if you had an address on him in San Valdesto."

He shook his head. "I didn't even know he had our address until about a week ago. I took him up there. I was glad to see him go." He took a deep breath. "But murder—?"

"He must have been very close to your father."

"Oh, yes! Those two deserved each other." He turned off the hose. "Mom is at work but I could make you a cup of instant coffee."

"There's a Big Boy restaurant only a few minutes from here. Let me treat you."

"I'd better put on a shirt," he said.

Over our cheeseburgers he told me that his sister was finally free of her nightmares after two years of psychiatric treatment. His mother was doing well as the manager of a local savings-and-loan institution. And his Uncle Charles had never, to his knowledge, owned a car. He had either borrowed one or bummed a ride.

"He *stole* Jane Meredith's," I pointed out. "If you ever learn his address, phone me."

He nodded. "If it's in San Valdesto. If it's somewhere else, I'll phone the police in that town. A murderer! Thank God, he didn't stay in our house overnight. He told me he had a job waiting for him in your town."

"It wasn't a job, it was a mission," I said. "He came there to kill me."

I stopped in at the hotel on the way back but Harley wasn't there. He was out in front with Corey when I came home.

114

"Anything new?" Corey asked.

"Only that we don't have to go hunting for that Toyota truck any more." I gave him the gist of my conversation with young Glen Turbo.

Harley said, "Mrs. Casey has invited me for dinner. I'll be going home from here. My wife phoned this morning and informed me that she will be having an operation the day after tomorrow. I want to be there before she goes to the hospital."

"Serious?" I asked.

"Serious," he told me, "but not dangerous. A hysterectomy. We had this forlorn hope that maybe we could have another child, though she's forty years old. But now—? Shit!"

There was a silence for seconds before he added, "I hope you get that creep, Brock."

"We'll get him, one way or another," I promised.

"I hope it's your way."

"One way or another," I repeated.

CHAPTER 15

ONE ALLY WAS GOING HOME. WE HAD A new recruit in Ventura. An army of professionals and a band of vigilantes were now trying to find one nitwit crapshooter with no success so far. How long could it last? And if he was finally captured would the police have a strong enough case to take into court? The burden of proof was on the prosecutor, as it should be under our Constitution. They could get him a couple of years for car theft (maybe). And then he would be out again. And this nightmare could start all over again. As a citizen, I should have been hoping the police would make the collar. As a victim, my last best hope was riding with the vigilantes.

I didn't voice these thoughts at dinner. Dialogue flowed around me; I didn't contribute. I was still wondering if the person who had driven Charles Turbo to Santa Monica was a San Valdestan. There was, of course, a possibility that he had taken the bus. But that would have exposed him too much to public view.

But so had the Valley Intruder been constantly exposed to public view and the hunt had been long and his capture a tactical error; he had wandered into an area of people who had very little reason to trust the courts for gringo justice. *They* rarely had a jury of their peers.

116

Mrs. Casey went up to her room after dinner. Harley got ready to leave. I didn't suggest it would be safer if he had a night's rest before leaving for home. Nor did I tell him to *please* drive carefully. He is almost as bullheaded as I am.

Jan and I walked to the car with him. On the way back to the house she said, "He is one handsome gent, isn't he?"

"I guess. He could use a few more pounds. And he's kind of slow on his feet. I really clobbered him in a run on the Santa Monica beach."

"You?"

"Yes, dear."

"What were you two doing on the Santa Monica beach?"

"I told you. We were running."

"And maybe looking for some feminine company?"

"Of course not! We had some offers, naturally. But we told the girls we were married."

"I'll bet you did!"

I shrugged. "Believe it or not. That's the way it was."

Opposing linemen and jealous women, I had learned through the years, stay more tractable if you can keep them guessing.

Chief Chandler Harris phoned me around nine o'clock. He said, "Brock, I think it is time you and I had a little talk."

"About what?"

"We'll discuss that when you get here. Could you be in my office at ten o'clock tomorrow morning?"

"I'll be there."

It was Mr. Callahan the last time I had been in his office. I was now Brock again. Cunning Chandler Harris had put on his Dale Carnegie mask. He was about to win friends and influence people. Or try to.

"Who was that on the phone?" Jan asked.

"Just one of those girls from Santa Monica who can't take no for an answer."

"Stop talking nonsense! I'm not in the mood for it."

117

"It was Chief Harris. He wants me to come to his office tomorrow for a strategy conference."

"Are you telling me the truth?"

"Not exactly, perhaps. He told me he wanted to talk with me. As you well know, it won't be the first time I have worked with the police in this town—and helped them. But it is also possible that he simply wants to lecture me."

"Why don't you phone Bernie and find out which it is?"

"I'll talk to him when he picks you up tomorrow. I've had enough talking for today."

Corey had already gone to bed. Jan read in the living room. I went over my records again, hoping to find some hoodlum I had helped bring to justice in San Valdesto, some local who might have driven Charles Turbo to Santa Monica. I found none who seemed likely.

It was a quiet breakfast, a gloomy breakfast, with an occasional mutter from Mrs. Casey.

I went out with Jan when Vogel came to pick her up. I asked him if he knew why Harris wanted to talk with me.

"I didn't know he wanted to," he said. "He didn't mention it to me. Now, remember he's my boss and he knows you're my friend. So try to use some tact for a change."

"I'll try, but it's not easy with him."

Chief Harris stood up from behind his desk and offered his hand when I entered. I shook it and sat down in the nearest chair.

He sat down and stared past me for a few seconds. "As you probably know, Brock, the Chicano element in our town resents me for some reason I have never understood."

"I know that," I agreed. "How many Chicano officers do you have in the department?"

He frowned. "Three. That's how many qualified."

"Sheriff McClune has eight."

"It's possible their standards are less strict than ours."

"It's possible," I agreed. *McClune's lack of bigotry could be one of the standards,* I thought.

118

"But you," he went on, "have been their benefactor, supporting both the Brotherhood and the Tomorrow Club."

The Tomorrow Club was a youth organization. I nodded.

"I have been informed by one of our undercover officers," he said, "that they are now getting involved in this search for Charles Turbo. Did you know about that?"

I lied with a shake of the head.

"Last night, before I phoned you, a man was severely beaten in the Diaz Hill area. He is now in St. Mary's Hospital with a broken arm and serious facial contusions. He refused to tell us anything except that it was Chicanos who attacked him. He is a—a black man."

I asked, "Are you suggesting that he might confide in me?"

"No, no! What I had hoped was that you might tell your Chicano friends to calm down. We suspect that the attack on this black man might somehow be connected to this case. And I hope you won't be offended, but I suspect their reason for this vendetta is their regard for you."

"It's possible," I agreed. "I'll talk to one of them. I'm sure you and I share a dislike for vigilante justice."

"I sincerely hope so."

"As we both know," I said, "there has been trouble ever since the blacks began to move into the Chicano neighborhood. But that is not true at the Tomorrow Club. They get along very well there. If this black man knows about my sponsorship there, perhaps he would tell me some things he would not tell a police officer."

He gave that a few moments of thought before he said, "Information you will, of course, relay to us?"

"Of course."

The man's name, he told me, was Davis Washington. He was in room 314 at St. Mary's Hospital. That wasn't far from the station; I walked there.

Davis Washington was in a double room, but the other bed was not occupied. He had a cast on his right arm and bandages swathed the upper part of his face. He was short and thin. He stared at me through the peepholes in the bandages.

"My name is Brock Callahan," I opened.

"The football player?"

I nodded.

"Didn't you room with Jugger Johnson?"

I nodded again.

"There weren't many white guys in those days who had black roomies."

"I know. But things have changed."

"Not enough of 'em. What do you want from me?"

"Any information you might have on Charles Turbo. He came to this town to kill me."

"Charley? You're crazy, man!"

I shook my head. "He's the crazy one."

"Why would he want to bump you?"

"Because I was responsible for putting his brother in jail. And he never got out. A couple weeks before he was up for parole he was stabbed to death by some of the inmates."

"Glen?"

I nodded.

"That could put Charley over the edge," he admitted. "Glen was the smart one. He got Charley out of a lot of scrapes. He kept him out of the can a couple of times, I remember, when he was picked up for assault. He never even got charged." He paused. "But murder?"

I said, "It's a ninety-nine-to-one bet he killed a kid in town here and a woman in Santa Monica."

"Jesus!" He took a deep breath. "When those Chicanos cornered me last night they didn't tell me anything about that. I told 'em to get lost and they went bananas."

"You told them nothing else?"

"I told 'em. *After* they went to work on me. And then they warned me if I beefed to the law, I'd get even worse than I had."

120

"What did *you* tell *them?*"

"I told 'em I picked up Charley about a week ago at the Travis Hotel. He offered me fifty bucks to drive him to Santa Monica. I drove him there. He was living with some woman down there. I never met her. I dropped him off in front of the house and headed for home." He stared past me. "If Charley has really gone heavy, be careful, footballer! Glen had the smarts, but Charley is the tricky one. He'll hit you when you least expect it."

"That woman's name was Jane Meredith," I told him. "She is the woman he murdered. The Santa Monica police agree with me on that."

"Christ! I could be tied into the mess if the Chicanos tell the local law."

"They won't and neither will I. Do you know of any other address Turbo had in this town?"

"I don't know the address. But when I picked him up once before he was at a rooming house near that Chicano bar on Padre Street. It's an old two-story house with shutters on the windows. He's probably long gone from there."

"Maybe and maybe not," I said. "Thanks."

"You'd better take a gun along," he said. "He's a hell of a lot bigger than you are."

I smiled, shook my head, and left.

The house he had described as a rooming house no longer was. It was apparently deserted. A sign on the parched gray grass of the small front yard informed any passersby that it was for sale or rent.

I took my lug wrench out of the rear deck and walked up the steps to the sagging porch. The door was locked. I went around to the back door. This, too, was locked. But it was a very flimsy door. I kicked it open.

I heard the sound of somebody moving on the floor above, the scrape of a foot. I went through the kitchen and down a narrow hall to the foot of the stairs. It was darker up above;

the window in the wall at the top of the stairs was tightly shuttered.

Silence. If it was Turbo, he had two options. He could come down these stairs or jump out of a second-story window.

More silence. And then a voice asked, "Al, is that you?"

"Come down and find out," I said.

"Callahan?" he asked.

I didn't answer.

The scrape of a foot again and suddenly he showed. Even in the dim light I could see his bald head and the scar.

"Callahan!" he said. "What's that you're carrying, peeper?"

"Protection," I said.

"It's not enough." He started slowly down the steps.

His hands were hanging at his sides, free of any weapon— until he was halfway down. His hand went into his right pocket and pulled out a small revolver. It looked like a .22-caliber purse gun. But it was more weapon than I had.

I threw the lug wrench at him before he could pull the trigger. It missed him. His first shot whistled past my left ear. I headed down the hall toward the back door. He leaned over the banister to get off a second shot at me. It missed. I was in the back yard before he could get off a third try.

I took the chance he would not show a weapon when he came outside. This was a crowded neighborhood. When I came to the side yard I saw him running up Padre Street. He turned at the next corner and was out of sight.

The Chicano bar Washington had mentioned was Rubio's. I phoned the station from there and asked for Vogel. I didn't want any of the other officers there to know what a fool I had been. I told him the story.

"You could have phoned us after you talked with Washington," he pointed out. "He'd be in custody now."

"I should have. But it was a doubtful tip."

122

"Okay! It will be our secret. I'll send out the word."

Rubio was arguing with a disgruntled horseplayer when I came to the bar. He smiled at me and said, "Pancho!" He glared at the horseplayer, pointed at the door, and said, "Go!"

The man left. Rubio asked, "What's on your mind? You look grouchy."

"I am, a little. That black man your *compadres* put into the hospital last night was telling you the truth."

His smile was cynical. "All of it? Did he tell you that he sells dope to kids and pimps for teenage whores?"

"No."

"Then let us start over."

"Let's. As I have told you before, the Brotherhood is not the law in our town."

"It is not the *gringo* law," he admitted. "But you must remember that we were here long before you *gringos* came to this country. And then your people thought it was India. We are far better friends of yours, Pancho, than most of the officers at the police station. Is that not true?"

"It's true," I said wearily, "I'll have a beer."

He put a bottle of his premium beer on the bar and a glass. "On the house," he said. "Trust us, Brock."

What other choice did I have? I nodded.

CHAPTER 16

RUBIO HAD HIS RIGID CODE; STAN NOWICKI, its reverse. Rubio's code was an-eye-for-an-eye vengeance, Nowicki's pure constitutional justice. The dichotomy was that when Rubio's underprivileged friends were victims of injustice it was Stan who fought their battles in court. Most of them couldn't afford the big-money boys.

Bernie and I held one belief in common; we hated to see the guilty walk early, many of them released on some technicality before they were even brought to trial. Where we differed was in method; I was forced to be more devious, lacking official status.

It was now one o'clock but perhaps Bernie hadn't gone to lunch at his normal time. I went to the station.

He had brought his lunch and Ellie, as was usual, had packed more than he could eat. I offered to share it with him, corned-beef sandwiches on dark rye bread.

He said, "I sent out the call. No answer so far. Harris told me this morning that you two are now bosom buddies."

"Not quite."

And McClune, he informed me, had phoned to tell him there had been a burglary in Omega last night. A motorist, going past, had seen the man leaving the house in the glow of his headlights. It had been a big man with a scarred cheek.

124

"Bald?" I asked.

"He was wearing a hat. If it's the man we want, why would he burglarize a house in the low-rent district? He picked up five hundred dollars in Santa Monica."

"He's a crapshooter and a bad one," I said. "Maybe he lost his wad in a local game."

"Maybe. Are you holding up all right?"

"So far. But when I think of all the trained and untrained hunters on that bastard's trail— And we've come up with nothing!"

"We've come up with plenty, you with the most. We need you, Brock. Stay healthy."

"I plan to. That's the nicest thing you've said to me in months. Thanks for the lunch. I think I'll run out to Omega and scout around. There's no way that man can operate without some local allies."

Bernie nodded. "He can't stay lucky forever. Keep the faith."

Harley had cruised the Omega streets and learned nothing. I cruised for over an hour with the same lack of success. I considered going over to visit The Judge while I was in the area. But Larry Rubin's recently purchased house was not far from here, out near the university. I drove there.

The former owner had built a one-room, bath, and kitchenette guest house in the rear which was now Larry's office.

I entered without knocking; his door was open. He was on the phone; he waved at me and pointed to a chair.

He seemed to be having the same trouble with his caller that Rubio had been having with his bar patron, a disgruntled horseplayer.

He hung up, finally, and shook his head. "Have you ever noticed that the richer people are, the slower the pay?"

"That was my experience in Los Angeles," I agreed.

"Did you come to bet or to talk?"

"I came to ask you if you have had any contact with crapshooters since you moved here."

"Only those who bet on the ponies. If it's Turbo you're thinking about, it isn't likely he'd have the scratch to mix with my clientele."

"He brought at least five hundred dollars with him when he came here from Santa Monica."

Larry smiled. "The way he plays that should last him about five minutes in a big-money game."

"I had the same thought. That might be why he burglarized a house in Omega last night."

"It could be. Brock, the way it reads to me, that guy is waiting for you to make a dumb move. You're protected at your house. So he has to get you out in the open. But first he wants you to know *why* he intends to kill you. He must have guessed you know by now and that will be his twisted revenge. I hope to hell you're carrying a gun."

"I'm not. What makes you think he knows what I have learned about him?"

He shrugged. "Like you, I go by my instincts. He's led you a merry chase. He knows some of the people you talked to in Santa Monica, not all of them solid citizens. It is time for you to get a gun."

"I have one."

"Well, damn it, carry it!"

His phone rang. He picked it up, listened, and said, "Two hundred on the nose. You're covered."

He cradled the phone and asked, "Are you going to carry the gun?"

"I'm thinking about it."

"Thinking is not your strong suit, Brock. Mine, either. And it sure as hell isn't his. Carry the equalizer."

"If you insist."

The phone rang again. I left.

Larry was probably right. Turbo and I were heading for showdown time and he wanted me on his ground. I didn't want him on mine, not with Jan and Mrs. Casey living there.

126

I took over for Corey in front when I came home so he could get come exercise. He left his gun with me.

Our new neighbors must be wondering what was going on across the street from them. It was possible Bill Crider had hurried out of town before he could get a fair price for his house once he saw the guard car in front of ours. This was ridiculous and demeaning. It was also expensive. What if I hadn't been able to afford it?

Patience, I told myself.

But patience, like thinking, is not my strong suit. And what did we have on Turbo that would stand up in court? As Bernie had pointed out, there were no witnesses to either murder. There was no weapon to incriminate him. What could he be charged with? Creating a public nuisance? Putting Jasper Belton on drugs, if proven, might get him a couple months in jail. But would Fernando Valdez, the garage guitarist in Santa Monica, testify against him? Not unless he could find some place to hide after the trial.

McClune phoned right before dinner to tell me he hadn't been able to find any record on Charles Turbo. The DMV didn't have a record of his ever having a driver's license.

I asked him about the motorist who had seen the man resembling Turbo leave the burglarized house in Omega.

"We don't even have his name," he told me. "He phoned in the information. It could be another of Turbo's tricks."

"Or maybe the man who phoned had reason to fear him."

"Maybe. There are too damned many maybes in this case."

"Vogel thinks it's possible we don't even have a case."

"It's highly possible. As an officer of the law, I shouldn't say it, but I hope the bastard resists arrest if we ever find him. I almost hope he takes the first shot—if he's armed."

"And misses," I added.

"And misses. Don't you dare ever quote me on that!"

On the tube the bad guy always takes the first shot and misses. This gives the good guy a moral excuse for killing the bad guy. In the real world both the good and the bad are

127

subject to legal appraisal of their acts and quite often it is the intended victim who winds up on trial. That includes a number of police officers, our guardians of the law.

In the military, if you kill enemy soldiers, you don't go on trial for it; you often get a medal. Is it possible that criminals are not our enemies?

Jan came home looking haggard. "Anything new?" she asked.

I shook my head.

"I don't know how much more of this I can take," she said. "Maybe we should move to Sun City."

"He'd follow us. I'll make you a drink."

I took a bottle of beer out to Corey first. When I brought our drinks, Jan had her shoes off and was half dozing on the couch.

"Would you like to take a nap first?" I asked.

"No. I need the calories. I've already lost six pounds."

She was asleep fifteen minutes later. I went out to sit with Corey.

He said, "I can't believe he's ever going to show here, not while the house is guarded."

"He has to show somewhere and there are a lot of people out hunting him."

"So the cops catch him and the judge sets him free or sentences him to a couple of years. What do we do then, start this all over again?"

I said nothing.

"One thing I've decided," he said. "If he ever shows here I'm not going to aim for his knee."

"If he spots you and runs don't shoot at his back. Because then *you'll* wind up in court. Do you want another beer?"

He shook his head. "My stomach's riled enough already."

Harley phoned after dinner and I told him all I had learned since he left town.

"I've thought about coming back there a couple of times," he said. "But finally decided not to."

128

I told him that Jan had suggested we move to his town.

"In that case I'd stay here. My wife and I have agreed that if we move back to California it won't be San Valdesto. Maybe San Diego. I was based there for four years and a lot of my Marine buddies are retired there."

"It's a good town to live in. I'll let you know if we have any luck here."

"I wish you had said *when* instead of *if.*"

"When," I said.

I took my transistor radio with me (and my gun) and went out to sit with Corey. We didn't talk much; we were talked out. We listened to a local radio station that featured the blended sounds of the big-band era and watched the cars go by on the road.

At nine-thirty I suggested he go to bed and get some extra sleep; I would stay out here until the guard came.

He shook his head. "I'm not sleeping well. This is just as restful."

"Maybe you need a respite, Corey. I could hire a guard for this shift and you could take some time off."

"No. I'll sweat it out with you. This isn't any duller than being staked out all night in my aunt's store in Los Angeles. I see you've decided to carry your gun."

"I have. In case you take the first shot—and miss."

"What a macabre thought! That's not funny, Brock."

"It wasn't meant to be. Let us remember that Turbo is not a kid robbing a music store."

The eleven-o'clock news on the tube from Los Angeles informed Jan and me that a total of two hundred prosecution charges had now been dropped as not evidential in the year-old trial of the child-molestation case against the nursery school.

The afflicted parents had held a mass protest meeting. They had voiced some possibly libelous remarks to the media reporters about the abusive defense tactics in the case, several of their words being bleeped out as probably pornographic. The most law-abiding citizen can turn into a vindictive vigilante when *his* or *her* child is involved.

The next juicy item concerned a pro-life group that had rioted in front of an abortion clinic.

"That's enough," Jan said.

She turned off the set and we went to bed.

CHAPTER 17

A SLIGHT TREMOR JUST AFTER DAWN awakened us. I turned on the bedside radio. A few minutes later we learned it had been a 3.7 quake, its epicenter about fifteen miles off the Ventura coast. Our big one was yet to come. Every Eden has its snake.

Jan said, "Next week, Armageddon. I can't sleep. I'm going down and make a cup of tea."

"I'm going with you."

We were about halfway through our tea in the kitchen when Mrs. Casey came in to make breakfast for Corey.

I suggested, "Why don't you two take a vacation? Hawaii should be fun. Or maybe Carmel?"

Mrs. Casey shook her head. Jan said, "We're not the ones he's threatening, Brock."

"Anybody close to me is in danger. The man is not sane!"

"We know that," Mrs. Casey said. "Look what he did to Corey. He could have killed him! But we belong here and we'll stay here."

There had been another quake in Mexico City, the morning paper informed me, 5.5 on the Richter Scale. A hurricane was heading for the Florida coast. Maybe Jan's awakening jest had some substance; we could be zeroing in on Armageddon.

131

It was a gloomy day, a cold damp breeze drifting in from the ocean. I was at a dead end now. What could I do but wait?

I didn't wait long. Half an hour later the desk clerk at the Travis Hotel phoned. He said, "Your friend Sarge asked me to call you. He's in trouble."

"With the police?"

"Not this time. With your Chicano friends. They cornered him in the Alamo Café last night. They didn't rough him up much, but he's scared, man! He's locked up in his room with a bottle."

"Okay. I'll come down. But first I'll make a visit to the Brotherhood. I'll straighten them out on that."

"I wish you would. And while you're there, put in a word for us black guys, too. Explain to Ricardo and his hotheaded friends that we are not *gringos*. They put Davis Washington into the hospital."

"I know. But, besides being black, Davis is a pimp and a drug dealer."

"That," he said, "I didn't know. Luck."

Brother against brother, sister against sister, people of all countries, colors, and religions fighting each other, hating each other, killing each other, when we all belonged to the same human family. Maybe Armageddon was overdue.

The headquarters of the Brotherhood was a small weathered stucco building, a converted store. The door opened directly into the meeting room, a square room furnished with about fifty folding chairs. The small office of Ricardo Cortez, head honcho, was partitioned off in one corner.

His door was open. He was sitting behind a chipped blue-enameled steel desk. He is an enormous man with a full gray-streaked black beard and bushy bone-white eyebrows.

He smiled at me. "You're angry about something, aren't you?"

"Yes. About what happened to one of my informants last night. I understand some of your soldiers roughed him up."

132

He shook his head. "Not quite. They questioned him. I am sure he has no bruises to support his claim. You know, of course, that he is also a police informant."

I nodded. "And that puts him on the right side of the law. Do I have to remind you, Ricardo, that when I saved you from a spell in jail I also worked within the law?"

He smiled again. "I'm sure you did, because you say so. Did you work within the law in Los Angeles, too?"

He had me there. I said, "When I could afford to."

He leaned back in his chair. "Brock, it is because of what you did for me and several of my people that we are now trying to repay our debt to you. We have no personal interest in this Turbo creature. He is not a local man and none of our concern. As for the police, how much have they helped you? How much have *they* learned?"

"Not as much as I did on my own," I admitted.

"Nor as much as we have learned," he added.

"Something I should know?"

"Nothing you will learn from us. We don't plan to involve you. We don't want our best gringo friend to go to jail. You can tell your informant we will not bother him again. He was told last night but he was probably too drunk to understand."

"I guess he still is. I'll have the desk clerk explain it to him when he sobers up."

"Do that. And one more thing you should consider. If the police finally catch this man and he goes to jail, how long will he stay there? And when he gets out, won't he have even more reason to hate you?"

"I suppose. Yes. But still—"

"I've said enough. Too much. I think it would be best for both of us if we forgot we ever had this conversation."

I said nothing.

He said, "We live in separate worlds, *amigo.*"

"Yes," I agreed. "I'll stop in and tell the clerk to give the word to Sarge."

Which I did and then went home.

The sun had come out. Corey was in the shade at the side of the house. He said, "You sure left in a hurry. What happened?"

"One of my stoolies was in trouble."

"That's all?"

"That's all!"

He looked at me suspiciously. "Am I too young to know?"

"Of course not!"

I stretched out on the grass beside his chair, bone weary from tension and frustration. All those miles, all those questions had added up to nothing. I had learned the man's name and his motive. I had learned everything about him except where he was hiding and when he planned to make his move. I might never learn where he was hiding. All I could do was hope I was ready when he made his move.

Patience . . .

I was dozing when Corey said, "It's time for lunch, Brock."

Mrs. Casey had set the card table for three in the shadow of the garage. It was a quiet meal.

Mrs. Casey had gone into the house and I was sitting with Corey when we saw and heard an ancient battered Volkswagen screeching around the bend below the house. It was out of sight for a few seconds before it topped the crest. When it reappeared we could see there were two long-haired young people of indeterminate sex in the front seat.

The right front window was open. Something came flying out of it as they sped past. It landed on our lawn. My first thought was *a bomb*, but it wasn't. It was a dead sea gull.

We were still staring at it when we heard the wail of a police siren on the road above the house.

"The damned creeps!" Corey said. "I hope that siren means what I think it means."

"It could be," I said. "I'll phone the station later."

I put the bird in the rubbish can and covered it with leaves. There were no marks on it; it must have died of old age.

134

Corey said, "It could have been picked up on the beach. Is that a clue?"

"Clue for what?"

"For where Turbo's hiding out."

"It might have been just a couple of kids who wanted a change from knocking over mailboxes."

"A coincidence? First the cat and then this? Brock! Why don't you phone McClune and tell him what happened here? Then he'll have more reason to pick 'em up."

I phoned McClune and told him what had happened and about the siren we had heard. He told me there had been no call from the car yet. He would let me know if one came in.

He called back fifteen minutes later. He told me the boys were being held and could I identify them? I told him I couldn't but it was possible Corey could. I went out to ask him.

"Both of them, and also the car," he assured me. "I'll go up to the station."

I took over his seat in the shade. I sat and sat and sat. Two hours later I phoned the station. McClune told me Corey and a deputy had gone out to upper Omega Beach. Corey had pointed out to them that upper Omega Beach could be the most deserted beach in the country since the oil spill several months ago from the offshore platform had made it repugnant to sight and smell. The boys had claimed that was where they had met this man who gave them twenty dollars to drop the sea gull on our lawn.

"Did they have a description of the man?"

"Hell, no! They came up with the phony story that they were sitting around a campfire out there last night when this man called them into the shadows. They're both lying."

"They're scared," I said. "They have reason to be."

"Probably. Then Corey remembered that refreshment shack out there has been closed since the oil spill. That's where he and the deputy are now."

"Are you going to hold the kids?"

"As long as we can. Both of them had their driver's licenses taken away months ago. Maybe they'll change their minds after they sit a while. You know, Brock, that Corey is one sharp lad. I wish he'd come to work for us."

"Not Corey," I said. "He's all free enterprise, just like me."

"Sure. But he hasn't got a dead rich uncle."

"He won't need one," I said, and hung up.

Corey came back half an hour later. He and the deputy had gone over the refreshment shack carefully. The door had been forced open, the padlock still hanging on the broken hasp. They had found two empty pork-and-beans cans and one empty Corinth cigarette package.

"He couldn't have been there long," I said, "unless he's a light smoker and a light eater."

"Right! But you know something we overlooked? We haven't checked out the stores in town that sell Corinth cigarettes."

"Corey, think of all the stores in this town that sell cigarettes! It would take us weeks to check out all of them."

"I know that. But how many wholesalers? I'm going to phone and find out."

McClune had called it right. Corey was one sharp lad.

When he came back from phoning he told me there was only one place in town that sold Corinth cigarettes, a Greek restaurant in Omega.

"You'd better tell McClune about it," I suggested.

"I just did." He sat down on the grass. "Do you think we ought to go out there?"

"Not me, Corey. I've done all the traveling I'm going to. I'm bone weary, man! That bastard has finally worn me down, just the way he planned it. The next move will have to be his. If he wants me he'll have to come and get me. This is my turf."

"I'll go out there," he said. "I know that scene. A lot of the kids I went to college with out there still live there. The young ones seem to be Turbo's best customers. I'm sure some are still on drugs."

"That could be," I agreed. "But this Turbo is no kid. He could be too much for you, Corey."

"Maybe not. I'm not a muscle man. But I'm only a couple lessons away from my black belt in karate. And I'm sure as hell strong enough to pull a trigger."

"Corey, damn it, you use your gun and you could wind up in jail again! You are not a cop. Remember that!"

He smiled. "I will. I owe you, Brock. My dad has been going to the office for me, picking up the mail and getting the messages from my answering machine. He told me he's picked up a couple of overdue checks. From here in, I work for free."

"All right! But keep in touch. Let me know where you'll be."

"Yes, Papa," he said. "I'll go in now and tell Mrs. Casey that I'm leaving. Don't tell her why."

"I won't."

CHAPTER 18

COREY LEFT. A LITTLE LESS THAN AN hour later Mrs. Casey came out to tell me he was on the phone.

The owner of the Greek restaurant in Omega, he informed me, had told him that a couple of long-haired kids had bought a carton of Corinth cigarettes several days ago. "They could be the two who threw the dead sea gull on the lawn."

"They could. Phone McClune."

"I did. He's sending a deputy to the restaurant with those two he's holding to see if the owner can identify them."

"What's the name of the restaurant?"

"The Athenian Café."

"I know where it is and I know the owner. I'll be out there as soon as I can get a guard here."

"You've decided not to sit and wait?"

"I have decided this is heavy enough for both of us. You were out of town when I worked on the case of the Greek hoodlum who was murdered."

"Chris Andropoulos? You told me about that case."

"I'll tell you more later. I have to phone for a guard."

By the time the guard arrived and I had driven to Omega, the deputy and the two youths were on their way back to the sheriff's station.

Corey was sitting in his car across the street from the café. The owner, he told me, had not identified the youths as the ones who had bought the cigarettes. He had explained that all long-haired kids looked alike to him.

"Did you learn their names?"

He shook his head. "It was one of their snotty deputies. He told me this was police business. How is the Greek here connected with Andropoulos?"

I told him how it was. He had worked for Andropoulos in Los Angeles. When Andropoulos was murdered he had come to town to take over his trade. He had run his book and sold his dope in the wrong end of town, the Chicano area. When he learned to his sorrow that it was hazardous to his health he had switched his operations to Omega.

"Let's go in and talk to him," I said.

He was sitting in a booth at the rear end of the place, drinking a cup of coffee, when we entered. He was a thin, short man with only a thin rim of black hair surrounding his bald pate.

He smiled at Corey. "Who's your friend?"

"My name is Brock Callahan, Mr. Dimitri. I am the man who helped put away the murderer of your good friend, Chris Andropoulos."

He nodded. "So I have been told, the former Ram. What can I do for you?"

"You can tell me why you lied to the deputy who brought those kids in."

He inclined his head toward Corey. "In front of a witness?"

Corey said, "I'll wait outside."

He left. Dimitri said, "Man to man, Mr. Callahan, I'm sure you can understand why I have no desire to cooperate with the police. Many of my young customers would desert me if I did. But I owe you and I'll be truthful with you. They were the same two."

"Thank you. Do you know their names?"

139

He shook his head. "I swear to you I don't. But the sheriff must have them at the station."

"That's true. May I use your phone?"

He pointed to a narrow door in the wall opposite the booth. "There's a phone in my office."

It was a small and cluttered room with a sweet aroma I could only guess about. Sheriff McClune, his secretary told me, had left the office an hour ago. He was on his way to a peace officers' convention in Los Angeles. He would be back tomorrow. Could she be of help?

I told her what I wanted. She gave me their names and addresses. I wrote them on a pad on Dimitri's desk. I asked her how long they would be held up there.

"They've already been released, Mr. Callahan. We had a big narcotics raid this morning and there was simply no place to hold them." A pause. "Oh, by the way, there's a message here Sheriff McClune left for Corey Raleigh, but I haven't been able to contact him. Do you know where he is?"

"Yes. He's with me."

"Would you please tell him that one boy we were holding also smoked Corinth cigarettes? We didn't learn that until a few minutes before he was released."

I thanked her and went out. Dimitri was having a cigarette with his coffee. A package of Corinth cigarettes was on the table next to his cup.

I asked him if the two boys were regular buyers of the brand.

"Not from me," he said. "I won't have that class of trade in my restaurant. Mostly, I get the college crowd, and most of them have stopped smoking."

I smiled. "Stopped smoking cigarettes you mean."

He returned my smile. "Yes."

Corey was sitting in his car. I handed him the slip. "Do you know where those addresses are?"

He nodded. I slid into the passenger's seat. "Let's go."

He swung the Camaro into a U-turn and headed toward

the university campus. He said, "That Dimitri is a real cutie, isn't he?"

"Oh, yes!"

"Before he took over that's where we used to get our grass."

"You—?"

"So I tried it and quit. This former classmate of mine got into the heavy stuff. That's where I'm staying out here."

"Are you paying him rent to support his habit?"

"It's not a him. It's a her. And she's not on any kind of dope now, light or heavy."

I made no comment.

"Don't tell Mrs. Casey I'm living in sin."

I didn't answer. We rode past the UCSV campus and turned onto a narrow pitted macadam road that led toward the marshland near the sea.

The residence of Frederick Norman Taylor was in a trailer park that bordered on the marsh. It was the smallest and oldest trailer in the park, and the only one without wheels, resting on concrete blocks.

A fairly stout but very pretty girl was standing near the doorway of the trailer talking with an older woman who was holding an armful of groceries. The woman walked away as we drove in.

"Mrs. Taylor?" I asked.

"Not yet," she said. "Freddie's not home, if that's why you're here."

"That's why we're here. Do you know where he is?"

"He told me he was going over to talk to a friend. He was only here for a couple of minutes. Are you friends of his?"

I shook my head. "We're hoping that he can help us find a man we're looking for, a man he might know."

She studied me suspiciously. "If you mean Al Gertz, he's not a man, he's a slimy creep! All he's ever done for Freddie was get him in trouble."

"I can believe it," Corey said. "We want to keep Freddie out of trouble."

She frowned. "Are you detectives?"

"Consultants," I said. "We're working with the sheriff's department."

She sighed. "Well, he's with Al now and I don't know where *he* lives."

"We do. Thank you."

"You're welcome. If Freddie's still there you tell him if he isn't back here in half an hour I'm taking off."

"I'll be sure to tell him that."

The address of Alvin Gertz was in a shoddy small-apartment-house area at the edge of the Omega shopping district. A thin, tall lad and a much bulkier one were about to climb into the cab of a battered Chev pickup truck on the parking lot when we arrived.

"The skinny one is Gertz," Corey told me.

"Just one minute, Al!" I called.

They both turned to stare at us. Al looked at Corey. "You again?"

Corey said, "We're looking for Fred Taylor. We were told he was here."

"You were told wrong. Get lost!"

His heavy companion smiled. "Is this the punk who was up at the sheriff's station when you and the wimp were there?"

Gertz nodded.

"Fatso," I said, "stay out of this! Our business is with Al."

"And Al's business is my business. You'd better leave, Pops, before you get hurt."

Maybe it was the *Pops* that did it or maybe the past days of frustration. He started toward me and I met him halfway. He swung a clumsy overhand right toward my chin. I moved inside of it and planted a left hand deep into his belly. He doubled up and I brought my right knee up sharply into his chin. It was the decisive shot. He went face down with a thump on the asphalt parking lot.

When I turned around, Al was reaching into the box of the truck. He pulled out a big crescent wrench—and Corey nailed him with a karate chop to the neck. The wrench went flying.

And then I heard the wail of a siren—and a sheriff's black-and-white pulled up on the lot.

Deputy Chief Clifton Adams is the man who runs the day watch at the station when McClune isn't there, a thin, tall, sour man. He looked at Corey and me and shook his head.

"What in hell were you two doing there, playing cowboy?" He looked at me. "At least *you* should know better. We were watching the place. We planned to follow the truck when it pulled out."

"I'm sorry. I blew it. What's the fat kid's name?"

"That," he said stiffly, "is police business."

Corey said, "Don't tell me you were going to follow the truck in a patrol car?"

Adams glared at him. "Of course not! That's a one-way street. The unmarked car was parked two blocks away. The patrol car was there to alert them when those two took off."

"I see," Corey said.

Adams continued to glare at him.

I said, "McClune gave me permission to work on this case, Cliff. And you know why. If he's in Los Angeles now, and you have a phone number where you can reach him, you can confirm that."

He took a deep breath and nodded. "There's no reason for me to phone him. He told me before he left to give you some leeway. But I'm sure you'll agree with me that he was not including vigilante action. Damn it, Brock, you should know that!"

"I should and I do. My only excuse is that I've had a lot of bad days lately. It won't happen again. As for Corey, he

143

saved me from getting brained. Gertz was about to dent my skull with a heavy crescent wrench."

He sighed. "I guess that's cause enough for action." He paused. "The fat kid's name is Adonis Rey. He's been in trouble before. He has a record. We're holding him, crowded as we are."

"He could be our lead to Turbo," I pointed out.

"Possibly. We'll hold him as long as we can. But somebody usually comes up with his bail. He must have connections. Okay, you can leave now."

We went out. Corey said, "If you ask me, I think it would be a hell of a lot smarter to keep the surveillance on the café instead of on those kids. Turbo could run out of messengers and have to make the trip himself."

"Good thinking," I said. "But Corey, you're going to have to learn to get along with cops. They're not the enemy."

"I know, I know! But, damn it, I get along with McClune!"

"That's probably because he doesn't have any kids."

He smiled. "Is that why I get along with you?"

"So far."

We climbed into his car. He said, "I'm going to keep an eye on that café. And I think I'll make another check of that deserted refreshment stand. Unless Turbo spotted the deputy and me when we were out there, he could have gone back. Do you want to come with me?"

I shook my head. "I want to go home and get a couple of belts into me. I feel as tight as a violin string."

He dropped me off at my car and gave me the phone number of the apartment where he was shacked up.

Is that why I get along with you? At the Tomorrow Club and with the Omega Little Leaguers, I worked with kids. God damn me and my male chauvinist jock pride . . .

Jan was mixing a drink when I came home. "You look like you could use a double," she said.

I nodded.

"Bad day?" she asked.

"Aren't they all?"

She sighed. "One double, coming up."

144

CHAPTER 19

I TOLD THE GUARD I WOULD AGAIN NEED round-the-clock service until further notice. I also told him to make sure all of the guards kept their cars concealed in the shrubbery bordering the driveway. Let Turbo think I was finally vulnerable.

I was in the shower, the massage spray on, when Corey phoned. He had gone back to the refreshment stand, he told me, and there was new litter in the place. "Three empty beer cans," he said, "and another discarded Corinth cigarette package. Jesus, that bastard is dumb!"

"Did you phone Adams and tell him?"

"Hell, no! He's got a surveillance on the café now. A real clever one, a black-and-white parked across the street! If I tell him about the stand he'll probably send two uniformed officers to sit in front of it. I can handle this."

"Corey, Damn it—!"

"Brock, I can handle this. There's a lot of heavy brush on the slope above the stand. I can watch it from there. There's a full moon tonight."

"And you plan to sit there all night?"

"Of course not! Until about midnight."

"Okay, okay," I said. "Luck."

He had called Turbo dumb. But Turbo had evaded the

police in Santa Monica and Ventura, in San Valdesto county and city. He had also not been located by any of the Brotherhood vigilantes. Dumb he might be. But damned lucky—except with the dice.

The moon came out, the night was clear. Jan and Mrs. Casey watched an old Paul Newman movie on the tube. I went back to read again my typed history of this sordid chase from the dead cat on the lawn to today's parking lot brawl.

Corey phoned around ten o'clock. "Another false alarm," he told me.

"What do you mean?"

He had walked to the beach from the apartment around eight. It wasn't far and he could think of no place nearby where he could hide the car. About an hour later, an ancient, battered Volkswagen Bug had parked off the dirt road above the beach. A couple had left it and started down the path toward the beach, carrying along a six-pack of beer.

"It was Al Gertz and some girl he didn't introduce me to."

"You talked with him?"

"I did. I remembered that McClune had told me both he and Taylor had lost their driver's licenses. I reminded him of that. He got snotty—and I showed him my gun. That cooled him."

"Corey, damn it—"

"No lectures, please. I asked him if he smoked Corinth cigarettes and he showed me his pack. I told him about Turbo and he swore to me he had never met the man unless it was the man who gave him twenty dollars at the beach to throw that sea gull on your lawn. He told me there was a possibility that Adonis Rey knew Turbo but he was sure Fred Taylor didn't."

"Maybe Rey and Gertz aren't as close as they seemed."

"It's the impression I got. I told him I wouldn't fink to the law about his driving without a license if he'd find out for me whether there was a Turbo-Rey connection. He said he'd try."

146

"I'll give you a hundred to your five he comes up with zilch."

"I know," he said wearily.

"You done good, Corey," I said. "Keep in touch."

"Yes, Papa," he said. He hung up.

Maybe Turbo had never inhabited the refreshment shack. That could have been a false lead. But then I remembered that there had been discarded pork-and-beans cans in the place. Young lovers seeking a sexual sanctuary would not be likely to bring those to their trysting ground.

The Paul Newman movie was almost over. I went in to sit with Jan and Mrs. Casey for the ten-thirty local newscast.

The opening story was the shocker. A youth named Frederick Norman Taylor had been found brutally beaten and unconscious in the tall grass of the Omega marsh. He was now in intensive care at the Omega Community Hospital. No other facts were known at this time.

When the newscast switched to other subjects, I phoned the sheriff's department on the phone in the kitchen. I knew the night commander. I identified myself and asked him if Adonis Rey was still in custody.

He was, he assured me. No bail bondsman had shown up so far.

Victim number three could now be chalked up to Charles Turbo, two young people and one old woman. I had trouble getting to sleep that night.

McClune phoned in the morning to give me hell. Cliff Adams had told him about the parking lot brawl. And also, he added, "I am almost ready to agree with your favorite police officer, Chief Chandler Harris, that your Chicano friends are beginning to be a problem."

"Somebody has to keep order in their neighborhood," I explained. "Harris never did."

"That is true. But now they are operating in my neighborhood and I don't like it."

"May I suggest that you send a couple of your Chicano

147

officers to a meeting of the Brotherhood? Those Brotherhood men are immune to *gringo* bullshit."

"Bullshit, me?"

"Bullshit, all gringos," I explained. "And probably they are even less likely to believe what a former Texan might tell them."

"You're walking a thin line, Brock."

"I'm saying what I think and you should know. What neither of us must forget is that we didn't earn this state, we *stole* it from them."

"I didn't steal it from them. I wasn't even alive then."

"That could be the theme your Chicano officers could stress when they go to the Brotherhood meeting."

"Dear God," he said. "The millionaire private eye now wants to be my public relations man!"

"Why not? You know how charming I can be."

"You bastard," he said, and started to laugh. "God damn you!"

"Keep the faith, friend. We're still friends, aren't we?"

"Yes," he said wearily. "But you're sure as hell crowding it. You keep me informed."

"Don't I always?" I asked—and hung up before he could answer.

I had another cup of coffee and drove out to the Omega Community Hospital. I identified myself as his uncle and the sweet young girl at the nurses' station informed me that Fred Taylor was still in intensive care but his prospects were brighter than they had been last night.

I was on the way out when Al Gertz came walking along the corridor from the entrance. He stopped to stare at me. "You?"

"Me," I admitted. "Your friend is still in intensive care. And the guy who put him there is the same man who paid you and Fred twenty dollars to throw that sea gull on my lawn."

He stared at me doubtfully. "What guy? You mean Turbo?"

148

"That's the man. Do you know him?"

He shook his head. "But I told your friend last night that maybe I could find him."

I took two twenties out of my wallet and handed them to him. "There's three more of those coming to you if you do." I gave him my phone number. "But you be damned careful! Turbo is wanted for murder, one here and one in Santa Monica."

"Man!" he said. "That's heavy!" He took a deep breath. "Your friend didn't tell me *that*. Are you sure he's the guy who—" He didn't finish.

"Beat up Fred?" I nodded. "And I'll bet your fat friend knows him."

"He's no friend of mine, not any more. And if I get too nosy with him I could wind up here, too."

"You could." I smiled. "Take your wrench along."

"That's not funny," he said. He looked at the twenties and back at me. He took another deep breath and said, "Okay, I'll try."

I drove out to the trailer park from there, to the trailer resting on cement blocks. The door was open. There was an old, worn leather suitcase and a tote bag on the ground near the door.

Fred's girl friend came to the open door as I got out of the car. "You're leaving him?" I asked.

She nodded. "He didn't come home last night. I warned him. Now I'm taking off!"

"He couldn't come home," I told her. "He's in the hospital. He's in intensive care at Omega Community."

"No," she said. "No! Is he—"

"The nurse told me he's improving. I'm sure he's going to make it. He was beaten up last night. Didn't anybody tell you?"

She shook her head. "Nobody. Damn it! The nearest bus stop is over a mile from here. Could you—"

"Put your luggage back in the trailer," I told her. "I'll take you to the hospital."

She started to cry when we were halfway there. There was nothing I could think of to say. When we got to the hospital I asked if she wanted me to wait and take her home again.

She shook her head. "I'm going to stay here until—" She wiped her eyes with the back of her hand. "Thanks for the ride."

It was eleven-thirty now. I went home to have lunch with Mrs. Casey. We had our prelunch libations as we always did when Jan wasn't home. It was a quiet lunch, and after we finished she went up to her daytime drama and I tried to read Jan's most recent intellectual book-club novel. It was not for me.

I decided to go down to Rubio's and relay to him the warning McClune had given me this morning.

CHAPTER 20

RUBIO WAS ARGUING, AS HE OFTEN DOES, with a customer at one of the tables. I don't know what the argument was about. English is the only language I know. His opponent was either losing or fed up with the discourse; he pointed at me.

Rubio turned and managed a smile. "Pancho!" He came over to stand behind the bar.

"I didn't mean to interrupt your conversation," I said. "What was it all about?"

He shrugged. "Nothing of importance. Who was it that said, 'at arguing, too, he owned his skill. For even though vanquished he could argue still'?"

"I don't know."

"Whoever he was," Rubio said, "I think he was talking about that deadbeat over there. Beer?"

I nodded.

He put a bottle of his finest on the bar and a glass.

I said, "I got a phone call from Sheriff McClune this morning."

His smile was cynical. "I can guess. Chicano justice, *gringo* law."

"Rubio, Sheriff McClune is *not* a bigot. He has quite a few Chicano officers working for him."

He poured himself a cup of coffee. "I know. Several of them are also working with us. And we're doing better than his department is."

"What does that mean—better?"

"Closer. Pancho, you are not involved in this. Let us talk of something else."

"Bear with me, please? As I told your president, this is not your town or my town. It is *our* town."

"You don't even live in town," he said. "And you don't know what it's like to live in this end of it."

"I don't? I've spent more free money in this end of town than you invested in this bar. That wasn't a very nice thing to say."

"It wasn't," he admitted, "and I apologize. And because you did what you did and are what you are, *nobody*, including our Holy Father, is going to stop us from finding your enemy."

"Finding—or destroying?"

His smile was even more cynical. He shrugged.

"Promise me this, if and when you find Charles Turbo, you will turn him over to the police."

He kept a straight face this time. "What else? Do you think we are outlaws? The beer is on the house. And now I must go over and apologize to my former friend. I forgot that he is still a customer."

Another wasted trip, except for the free beer. I finished it and went out. I drove through the mean streets to the freeway and headed for the Montevista turnoff.

I hadn't had much sleep the night before. I stretched out on the sofa in the den and tried to nap. I was awake and adding to my records when Jan came home.

"Nothing new, I suppose," she said.

"Nothing worth repeating."

"I'll make you a drink. It's the least I can do."

I shook my head. "My stomach is acting up."

"Some baking soda in water?"

I nodded.

It helped a little. So did Mrs. Casey's chicken soup. I phoned the hospital after dinner and learned that Fred Taylor was now out of intensive care.

"Another trip?" Jan asked.

"A short one. I have to visit a sick friend at Omega hospital."

"Anyone I know?"

"A kid. One of my Little Leaguers."

"I'll bet," she said. "Go!"

When I pulled into the hospital parking lot I saw an old Chev pickup truck at the far end. It looked to me like the truck Gertz and Rey were about to get into when Corey and I had come on the scene.

I parked near the entrance to the lot and walked in the shadows on the other side to get a closer look. There seemed to be nobody in the cab. Then, from the opposite entrance to the lot, a car drove in and its headlights illuminated the shadows on the far side. Adonis Rey was briefly revealed, leaning against the wall of the hospital, smoking a cigarette. He had finally found a bail bondsman.

I went back to my car and sat. About twenty minutes later, Al Gertz came out, revealed in the overhead light of the hospital doorway overhang, and walked down toward Rey. I started the engine.

The truck pulled out. I followed it down Laguna Street to the freeway entrance and down that to the freeway. I let a couple of cars get between mine and the truck. It went through town without having to stop for the lights. So did I.

About a quarter of a mile before the Montevista offramp, the truck moved over to the left lane. The Montevista turn-off, unlike most, led off the left lane. Was it possible they were heading for our house?

It was possible. The truck turned off onto our road. But it went past the house and continued its winding climb. The

153

memory of that night when Corey had been lured and framed came back. Was this another of Turbo's ploys?

That seemed unlikely. How could he have known I was going to visit the hospital tonight?

That Gertz! Taylor's sweet roommate had been right about him. He wasn't Fred's friend; he and Adonis were still allies. Gertz had conned both Corey and me.

It was a clear, bright night; I stayed at least one curve behind the truck. There was no traffic coming the other way when I headed into the final curve. I switched off the headlights and slowed the car.

The truck was parked in a hollow below the road. They left the truck and walked toward the shack where Jasper Belton had died. I drove past the crest and parked off the road in the shadows of a line of eucalyptus trees.

There was a possibility that Turbo was there or coming there. There was no light visible in the shack. That made sense; the county patrol boys would certainly investigate a light in a deserted shack.

If Turbo was there or coming there, I was naked. I hadn't brought my gun. Adonis I could handle, but not the three of them. I should have listened to that pushy salesman who had tried to sell me a car phone. This was a time to call the law.

I moved quietly down toward the shack, crouching in the high, dry grass and the thick chaparral. I could hear voices through the glassless window as I drew closer.

One I could recognize, the voice of Alvin Gertz. He said, "I talked with Taylor at the hospital. He told me he can't identify you. We brought that ammo you wanted. It's in the truck. We'd better get out of here."

And then a voice I didn't recognize. "Wait'll I finish this beer. We sure as hell don't want to get picked up for drinking in a moving car."

Damn it, if only I had brought my gun. . . . I moved as quietly and quickly as I could back to the car. I burned rubber going back to the house.

154

Jan was in the den. I used the kitchen phone to call the sheriff's department. I told the night man where they were and what I had overheard.

"I'll send out the call," he said. "I'll phone you if we pick them up. We'll need you for a witness."

When I went into the den, Jan asked, "How was your friend?"

"I never got to see him." I told her what had happened. "I wish to hell I'd had my gun with me."

"I'm glad you didn't," she said. "In the mood you're in? And remember, he could be armed, too. Let's just sit and hope." She turned off the TV. "Maybe some cocoa?"

We had the cocoa and waited. Nothing. At eleven o'clock I phoned the station. The commander told me neither Gertz nor Rey had been at home. Nor had the truck or the man I thought was Turbo been apprehended. "I'll phone you the minute we learn anything."

Jan went to bed. I stretched out on the sofa in the living room. I have no idea when I finally fell asleep. Jan had gone to work when Mrs. Casey came into the living room at ten o'clock to tell me Sheriff McClune was on the phone.

They had nothing. They were nowhere. The entire county had been alerted to watch for the Chev truck. Something had to break.

"I know," I said. "My sanity. I gave your warning message to Rubio yesterday. I wish I hadn't, now."

"Brock—!"

"I'm not in a mood for argument," I told him. "Let me know if you stumble onto anything interesting." I hung up.

Shortly before noon the guard came in to tell me he was coming down with the flu. Would I call the office for a substitute?

I told him to go home. I would take his place until the evening guard came. I got my gun and went to sit in the shadows in front of the garage door, hoping against hope that Turbo would show on my watch.

Mrs. Casey and I ate our lunch out there on a card table. Then she went up to her room. I sat and sat and sat.

Around three o'clock the sun began to work its way into my concrete paved sanctuary. I moved my station into the living room.

Corey came about fifteen minutes later. He looked embarrassed. The way it was, he explained, he had come up with nothing out in Omega. Would I be offended if he just finished out the day?

"Of course not! Did your girl friend throw you out?"

He shook his head. "I had a message on my answering machine when I checked the office this morning. I phoned the man from there. It's a—a—I mean, it could be a big-money case."

"Take it," I said. "You have my blessing."

"Thanks. Anything new on your end?"

"Nothing," I said. "If anything pops out in Omega before you leave there, phone me."

He nodded. "I think I'll just cruise the town and maybe talk with some of my former classmates."

He left.

CHAPTER 21

HARLEY HAD GONE HOME. COREY WAS spending his last day on the hunt. The Brotherhood's soldiers were probably scouting all the terrain between Montevista and Omega. And the man who had the most to win or lose was sitting and stewing. McClune's soldiers had come up with nothing. Something had to break, he had told me. Maybe . . . But it was probable my Chicano friends had more dedicated warriors in the field looking for Turbo than the sheriff's department had. His boys were putting in their eight hours. My friends were on a mission.

Vigilante justice or courtroom law? In my present mood, as the victim, I was rooting for the Brotherhood. It is not easy to be objective when you are the victim. If one of us was doomed to die I preferred that it be Turbo.

Vogel came over to talk with me when he brought Jan home. "What's your boiling point now?" he asked.

"About two degrees short of erupting."

"Harris has been complaining again about the activities of your Chicano friends."

"Tell him to hire some Chicano officers and maybe I'll listen to him."

"Brock, as you damned well know, I have complained to him about that. Often!"

"I know. I'll be okay, Bernie. Did Jan tell you what happened last night?"

He nodded. "One against three—and you unarmed. You could have been killed."

"It won't happen again."

"I'm glad to see you're getting some sense."

"Next time I'll carry the gun."

He shook his head. "You'll never learn, will you? I'm tired of arguing with you!" He stared at me for seconds and then turned abruptly and walked to his car.

Jan came out about five minutes later, bringing a bottle of beer for me and a diet Coke for her. She had become concerned about her weight again lately.

She sat in the deck chair next to mine. "Bernie," she said, "seems to think you have a death wish."

"I have. But it's not *my* death I'm wishing for."

She said nothing, staring out at the road. A sheriff's patrol car drove past slowly. The driver waved at us. I waved back.

Jan asked, "How long can they keep up the surveillance?"

"I don't know."

"Maybe I was wrong. Maybe you should have taken your gun with you last night."

"And maybe not. They were talking about ammunition. That can include more than bullets or shotgun shells. I might have nailed one of them—and been blasted into eternity by one of the other two."

"Let's not talk," she said wearily. "Let's just sit."

We were still sitting when Mrs. Casey came out to tell me I had a phonecall. It was a woman, she said.

It was a girl, Fred Taylor's live-in girl friend.

"How is he doing?" I asked her.

"Good. He's out of intensive care. He's going to make it. Al Gertz came to the hospital to visit him last night."

"I know."

"Well, that reminded Fred about a place where he and Al and their buddies used to throw some wild parties. He told me to phone Mr. Raleigh. I did but he wasn't home. Some woman there gave me your name."

"I'm Corey's partner. Where is this place?"

It was a deserted small house, she told me, at the end of a dirt road without a name. It led off Ridge Drive right opposite the pumping station at the Alcehama Reservoir.

"Should I have phoned the police?" she asked.

"Not yet. They might have been there already and it could be a wild-goose chase. I'll check it out."

"Isn't that dangerous?"

"Yes. Hold your thumbs."

"For you *and* Fred," she said. "Good luck, Mr. Callahan."

I told Jan to phone the guard service and tell the night man to come early. I told her to stay in the house and keep the doors locked. I had to see a man.

"We're eating in half an hour," she said. "What man?"

"A friend of Corey's. I should be back before dinner. If I'm not, eat without me."

"Brock—!"

"Damn it, Jan, I don't have time to argue. This could be important!"

"And dangerous?"

"No," I lied.

She stared at me as Vogel had. She took a deep breath and said, "I'll phone the guard."

A lie to be followed by a foolish move. . . . But the adrenalin was pumping in me. I had reached the eruption point.

The Alcehama Reservoir wasn't far from here, supplying the water for Montevista. Ridge Drive forked off our road two blocks below our house. Ten minutes later I turned into the rutted dirt road across from the pumping station and started the uphill climb.

This could be another of Turbo's ploys. It was possible that Al Gertz had intentionally reminded Taylor of the house at the hospital last night. He and Turbo and Adonis Rey must know by now that Fred Taylor was no longer an ally. The three of them could be waiting for me to show.

That was the reasonable thought. I'd had too many days of anger and frustration behind me to leave room for reasonable thoughts.

The house was a small weathered frame house set in a grove of eucalyptus trees. Two dead orange trees were in the front clearing. There was no Chev pickup truck nor any other vehicle in sight.

I pulled into the grove well short of the house and walked in its cover to the crest of the hill. On the far side, a quarter of a mile below, a small yellow sedan was parked on Solono Road. I couldn't tell from here if it was occupied.

There were two doors visible now, one on the side of the house, the other the front door. There was a pair of leaning laundry posts in the clearing at the side of the house. There might also be a rear door but the cover was too sparse to risk a look.

A house this small with *three* outside doors? And then the laundry posts reminded me that the side door could be the laundry room door, just as it had been in the small house I had grown up in in Long Beach.

That could be the safest point of entry. I took out my gun, stayed low, and headed for it.

The door was ajar. I pushed it open. It was a laundry room; I could see the galvanized iron tub. A stack of yellowed newspapers was in one corner, a three-year-old calendar on the far wall.

I waited, my heart pounding, my gun hand trembling, waiting for a sound, almost hoping the house was empty. But only almost. Up the one step and I was in the house.

The door in front of me now must open to a hall or a kitchen. A kitchen in the middle of the house? It had to be a hall. I turned the knob and started to open it.

The hinge creaked. I waited for a sound. None. I opened the door far enough to get a view of the other side. It was a hall. If the creep was in here he could be watching from either end.

A quick low glance revealed that he wasn't. The kitchen was at one end, a small dining room across the hall, the front door at the other end. The bedrooms must be on this side. The living room archway was visible from here, opening off the hall.

There was the drone of a plane overhead but not a sound in the house. Only a portion of the kitchen was visible but I could now see there was a back door. That gave me three exits—if the need should arise.

I turned toward the kitchen—and a voice from the other end of the hall said, "I'm here, Callahan!"

I crouched and turned and aimed, and almost pulled the trigger. But he was unarmed.

He stood there, grinning at me, big and bald and ugly. He said, "A tough footballer like you? This time you brought your gun, I see."

"I didn't come to kill you," I told him.

"No kidding? Why not?"

"I plan to take you to the law."

"How? You going to keep the gun on me with one hand and drive with the other?"

"There's room for you in my deck. Move it, creep!"

"You gutless bastard!" he said. "I figured you'd want it like I want it, man to man."

"Move it!" I repeated.

He shook his head—and stepped through the archway to the living room. Damn it! Why hadn't I pulled the trigger? He probably had an arsenal in there.

"Come on, gutless," he called. "I don't have no gun. Come and get me."

I thought of the dead Jasper and Jane Meredith being nibbled by rats and Fred Taylor now out of intensive care. It must have made me as loony as he was. I moved slowly to the living room archway.

161

He was standing at the far end of the room, still grinning, what looked like a grenade in his hand.

"Come in, sucker," he said. "I haven't pulled the pin. Not yet."

"Pull it and throw it," I told him, "and I promise you you'll die where you stand."

"And maybe you, too?" He nodded toward the front window nearest to him. "I'll put the grenade on the sill there. You put the gun on the sill of that window near you. Man to man, gutless?"

I could have shot him twice before he pulled the pin. But would it kill him? And *could* I kill him? Those were my rational thoughts.

I wasn't completely rational at the moment. I put my gun on the sill nearest me. He put the grenade on the sill nearest him. He made his move first, his arms dangling, his idiot's smile still on his scarred face as he came toward me.

Jesus—a wrestler! A groan-and-grapple yoyo. This shouldn't take long. Even underweight quarterbacks usually gave me more trouble than wrestlers.

When he was within reach his long right arm stretched out for my neck. I knocked it away with my left hand and put my right fist smack into the middle of his face. Blood spurted from his nose and seeped down from his lips.

The bastard didn't back up. He crouched and kept coming and slammed the top of his bald head into my belly. Weight was one thing he had going for him; I bounced back into the wall. He kept coming, still low.

He was still looking at the floor when I jammed my knee into his face. He went down and grabbed my left leg. I tried to kick him with my right leg; but my balance deserted me. I fell over him, rolled clear, and got back on my feet at the other end of the room.

He kept coming, head down, like a bull at a matador. I waited for his final charge—and made my matador move, stepping clear of his charge. He slammed headfirst into the wall, went down and rolled over.

He wasn't unconscious, not yet. He had strength enough to mumble, "You win, footballer."

"Get up when you're able to," I said, and walked slowly and painfully, my belly aching, to pick up my gun, my back to him.

I was almost in the archway when I heard the rattle on the floor behind me. That tricky son of a bitch . . . It was the grenade.

I was through the archway and out the front door before I heard the explosion.

Smoke drifted out from the door but the living room windows had not shattered. Was he still in there and alive? If he was, did he have a weapon? There was none in there I had seen. But how could I be sure?

I waited too long. The smoke was cleared out and the living room empty when I came back into the house.

I ran the length of the hall to the back door in the kitchen and opened it. Far down the slope a man was running, a big man, heading for Solono Road. The yellow sedan was still parked on the side of the road and a man heavy enough to be Adonis Rey was standing next to it.

I had been outwitted by a nitwit. Why hadn't I phoned McClune after Taylor's girl friend had given me the message? I sure as hell couldn't alert him now. What could I tell him? That Turbo's new transportation was a yellow sedan? The town was loaded with yellow sedans. Could I explain to him how I knew it? Never!

At home, Jan asked, "Did Corey's friend tell you anything I should know?"

"Nothing," I said.

"Your dinner is in the oven," she informed me. "Mrs. Casey and I didn't want to miss 'Fawlty Towers' on the tube."

She went back to the den. I poured a half tumbler of Mrs. Casey's Irish whiskey and had it with my warmed-over dinner. I have forgotten now what it was.

The man was still out there somewhere, waiting for another chance. Three of the chances had been mine and I'd lost all three. The next move he made could be the fatal one—for me.

Mrs. Casey and Jan were in the living room, playing gin rummy, when the phone rang at nine o'clock. I answered it. It was young Glen Turbo.

His uncle, he told me, had just phoned him and asked him to pick him up in San Valdesto early tomorrow morning. He had promised to pay him fifty dollars for the trip. Glen had assured him he would be there.

"What's the address?" I asked him.

"He told me to meet him at a Mobil station on the corner of Avon Road and Locust Street. He told me how to get there."

"I hope you don't plan to meet him there, Glen."

"Only if I had a gun, and I don't. *You* can meet him there."

I thanked him and went out to the living room. Mrs. Casey and Jan looked at me expectantly. "Good news?" Jan asked.

"I'm not sure. A lead."

"You said something about somebody meeting him there. What was that all about?"

"A possible informant," I told her. "I don't want to talk about it. I have some thinking to do first."

I went into the den, remembering the events of the day. I did have some thinking to do. It was decision time.

The station Glen had told me about was a *former* service station, now deserted. It was less than four blocks down the hill from our house. Charles Turbo could walk from there to here and back. He must have finally decided to make his move, now that the house no longer seemed to be guarded. He'd had other chances to get me, but not here, not at home.

It was possible he had planned all along to get me at home. And maybe Jan, too? He had left town only because the heat was on here. He knew where I was staying in Santa

Monica, but not in which room. The rest of the time Harley and I were there we had been constantly on the move, doubtful targets.

And here? I would be the victim—but Jan and Mrs. Casey could be witnesses. Would he let them live to identify him? No.

Decision time . . .

I could phone McClune and his boys could take over. If Turbo was armed and made the mistake of resisting arrest, if he decided to play shoot-it-out with the deputies, the threat to me would be diminished. They would finally have a case they could take into court and he would wind up where he belonged—in jail. Or dead.

If his irrational brain turned rational enough to accept the arrest, what would the prosecutor have? Car theft? That should get him a light sentence. They had no previous record on the man.

I could phone Ricardo Cortez and let the Brotherhood wreak their vengeance or take my trusty Colt down to the service station and play cowboy. That last could put me in jail or in my grave. The first would be a final solution to my problem. The soldiers of Cortez don't take prisoners.

It seemed clear to me that they were my best hope. But why should they risk their lives for me? This was my war, not theirs. To Sheriff McClune it would be another night of mayhem where some of his soldiers could be killed. From the conversation I had overheard between Gertz and Turbo, they were into the heavy ammo now.

I went out the back door and told the guard what I had learned tonight and what I feared. He said, "I'll watch the back and this side of the house. You can take the front and the other side."

"I'm not staying," I told him. "Can you get another man or two up here quickly?"

"I can have 'em here in five minutes. I have a phone in the car."

"Good. But don't use your guns unless you have to."

"I know what you mean," he said. "I learned that the hard way the first year I was with the agency. I was lucky. I had a good lawyer. I suppose you're going to take the women with you?"

I shook my head. "This is personal."

He was silent for seconds, staring at me. "I'll forget you ever said that. One man or two?"

"Two," I said.

He went to his car to phone. I went into the house to get my gun. In the living room I told Jan what young Glen had told me—but without telling her Glen was my informant. I also told her I had sent for two more guards.

"I'll be outside," I told her. "The more men the better. Somebody has to watch the back of the house."

"Mrs. Casey has gone to her room," she said. "I'll go up and sit with her. Aren't you going to phone the sheriff?"

"The guard will handle that. I'll come in when the deputies get here."

"Brock, you be careful!"

"Of course!"

I waited until the other guards came before I started walking down the hill to the Mobil station. The night was dark; I brought a flashlight.

What would it be this time with that slob, another grenade or a purse-size revolver? Why was I assuming he would be there? He could be watching our house right now or on his way to the station. He could be anywhere. He had told his nephew to pick him up early in the morning.

I knew the layout of the station; I had been a customer here before the owner had retired. There were two doors to the toilet, one opening into the garage, the other one to the outside.

The door that led to the office was on the side of the building facing the street, and there was occasional traffic tonight. I didn't want to be seen by any passing motorist.

When the road was clear I tried the office door. It was locked. I went back behind the building again before any headlights showed on the street.

The outside toilet door was not locked. That had to mean he was in here somewhere. But where? I opened the door slowly. A brief glow of my flashlight revealed that the toilet was vacant. I went in, gun ready, light out, and groped for the door to the garage. It was not locked.

That tricky bastard! He had probably conned his nephew into trapping me. He hadn't planned to be here tomorrow morning. He wanted *me* here *tonight*.

I took a deep breath, opened the door and stepped into the garage. I turned on the flashlight—and there he was, standing next to the far ramp, a sawed-off shotgun in his hands.

I turned off the flashlight as he lifted the gun and pointed it at me. I crouched low.

Then, from the direction of the office, a voice called out, "Don't pull that trigger, you *gringo* bastard!"

I saw the blast of the shotgun and heard the pellets ricochet off the wall above the office door.

I turned the flashlight on and put three bullets into Turbo, one in the stomach, two in the chest.

From the office, the voice called, "Good work, *amigo!*"

I swung the flashlight toward the office doorway. Too late. I heard the outside door that had been locked open and slam shut.

I could tell from where I stood that Turbo was dead. There was blood splattered all over the cement floor. Nausea stirred in me. I got out of there in a hurry.

Jan and Mrs. Casey were still upstairs. I phoned Sheriff McClune at his home and told him everything except for the assist of my unknown aide and the call from young Glen.

"You could have phoned us first," he said.

"After all the dead ends we've both run into? I was trying to save the taxpayers some money."

"I'll send an ambulance down there," he said, "and a couple of deputies. I'll be right over."

I went out and told the guards they could go home. They didn't ask me why. Maybe they knew.

Jan and Mrs. Casey must have heard them leave. They came down a few minutes later.

"What happened?" Jan asked.

"The threat is over," I told her. "Sheriff McClune is on his way here now to give me the story."

"Thank God!" Mrs. Casey said. "I'm going upstairs. I don't want to hear it."

Jan stared at me, sighed, and asked, "Should I stay?"

"If you want to."

She was sitting on the couch when McClune came. He said to me, "We'll go into your den." He looked at Jan. "Unless you have a strong stomach, I don't believe you'll want to hear what I'm going to tell Brock."

"I haven't had a strong stomach since all of this started," she said. "I'm almost glad the man is dead."

In the den, McClune asked, "Did Turbo shoot first?"

I nodded. "And missed. Could I call it a citizen's arrest?"

"You won't need to. I deputized you this morning. Who was your informer?"

"I don't know. I couldn't recognize her voice. That's why I didn't phone you."

He smiled. "Gad, I wish you were working with us."

"Haven't I always? And for free? That should help your budget."

"You have. I consider you a good citizen, Brock. Thanks."

"You're welcome," I said.

I went to the door with him and went back to sit with Jan in the living room.

"Peace at last!" she said.

I nodded. And the thought came to me that it isn't hard to be a good citizen if you have vigilante friends.

168